THE RETURN

Gruger had hardly reached his position when he saw his quarry coming. He knew the man as well as if a herald had gone before, announcing that this was Andrew Lanning. The bold, free step, the well-poised head, and something, moreover, of hair-trigger alertness about the man convinced him that this was the gunfighter, this was certainly the man of action.

Lefty slipped his hand into his coat pocket and ran the tips of his fingers lovingly over the familiar outlines of the automatic. He withdrew his hand, bringing out a cigarette box, and took out and lighted his smoke with his usual speed. He had snapped the match away, and it was fuming in the dust when Andrew Lanning came close.

"You're Lanning," he said smilingly, and held out his stubby hand. "I'm Gruger," he said, continuing the introduction. "I've dropped out here on a little piece of business with you. A sort of private business, Lanning. I've come out here to bump you off."

MAX BRAND

THE RETURN OF FREE RANGE LANNING

A WESTERN TRIO

LEISURE BOOKS NEW YORK CITY

A LEISURE BOOK®
August 1997
Published by special arrangement with
Golden West Literary Agency.

Dorchester Publishing Co., Inc.
276 Fifth Avenue
New York, NY 10001

THE RETURN OF FREE RANGE LANNING: A Western Trio by Max Brand™ was first published in book form by G.K. Hall & Company. Copyright © 1995 by Jane Faust Easton and Adriana Faust-Bianchi.

Further copyright information can be found at the end of this book.

Printed in the United States of America.

THE RETURN OF FREE RANGE LANNING

A WESTERN TRIO

TABLE OF CONTENTS

THE BLACK MULDOON

When Frederick Faust's "The Black Muldoon" was first published in Street & Smith's *Western Story Magazine* in the issue for September 30, 1922 it was under the byline Peter Dawson. In that same issue the sixth installment of a seven-part serial by Faust titled "Old Carver Ranch" was appearing under the byline John Frederick. It is probable that Frank Blackwell, who edited the magazine, provided the Peter Dawson byline for Faust for "The Black Muldoon" and it was the only time in all of his publishing career that a Faust story ever appeared under this pseudonym, the name of a popular brand of Scotch whiskey. Some fourteen years later when the first Western story by Jonathan H. Glidden was sold by his agent, Marguerite E. Harper, to Street & Smith's *Complete Stories*, where it appeared as "Gunsmoke Pledge" in the May, 1936 issue, Harper informed Glidden that the story would be published under the byline Peter Dawson. She later confided to Glidden that she had picked that name because she happened to be drinking that brand of Scotch at the time. Glidden went on to publish numerous novels and short stories as Peter Dawson. "The Black Muldoon," under whatever byline, remains a gripping narrative in which Faust explored the urgent question of what ultimately takes precedence in a person's life: nurture, genetics, psychology, character, temperament, or fate.

Chapter One
Jerry Muldoon Arrives

His day had begun at five in the morning, but eleven at night found Jefferson Peters still at work over his ledger. Sometimes, out of the upper story and rear rooms of the old crossroads hotel and general merchandise store, a piercing, small rhythm of sound worked down to him. Whenever he heard it, Jefferson Peters dropped his pen and folded his hands with nervous fingers and looked into the future with a falling heart. Upstairs were new-born twins, small, pink bodies possessed of strangely lusty lungs. Over them leaned Kate, his dear wife. Three lives depended upon young Jefferson Peters.

No wonder, then, that his stomach grew hollow and his throat man dry. The day when the minister pronounced them man and wife had been bad enough, for on that day he had taken upon his not overly broad shoulders the responsibility of another life. But that day was nothing compared with this. Two lives, although so new, two mortal souls although so lately come into the world—it seemed to poor Jeff Peters that their smallness was a dreadful thing. Out of his work their bodies must find the means to live and grow; out of his soul their souls must have sustenance.

A wan ghost of his face suddenly stared out at him from the wall. He saw colorless lips, a thin, pinched cheek, hollow eyes. It was his image in the little mirror which hung on the opposite wall; but, nevertheless, it seemed to Jeff Peters a ghost portentous of ruin and dismay. He stood up from his desk where he had labored so long and so futilely to make the figures for that month show a real profit and, lifting the lamp above his head, he looked eagerly about him.

It was a large room, filled with salable articles. He took heart at once. Yonder, blue and red and yellow rolls of ginghams and calicoes should clothe the figures of the women of the town of Custis sooner or later. There were sleek-barreled Colts to make the hearts of young cowpunchers jump, to say nothing of long, spoon-handled spurs, rifles and shotguns, ropes, boots, and a thousand articles of saddlery. In a far corner glimmered the steel blades of hoes and spades and shovels for those who kept vegetable gardens. There were augers for digging post holes, saws, hammers, barrels of nails.

Adjoining this came the hardware department where one could find anything from pairs of Dutch ovens to rolling pins. Beyond this, again, was the colorful and shimmering department of the little pharmacy, rich in patent medicines—a thousand bottles, and each with contents of a different hue. Every inch of the floor space was crowded with the necessaries of cow-country life. And from the very ceiling hung a myriad other things. Yes, there was a plentiful stock on hand, and it would sell at handsome prices. But, alas, it would not sell at all until the gala days of the fall roundup. Could he hold out that long? He lowered the lamp with a sigh, while the shadows swept across all the colors in his store and illumined no more than the one sharply defined circle upon the desk where he had been working.

There came a knock at the door, and Jefferson Peters jerked up his head in surprise, for the men of Custis had various bad habits, such as taking goods and failing to pay for them until two or three years later; but they had never yet shown a fondness for late shopping hours. Redeye was the only thing purchased after dark. It was probably someone who wanted a room for the night and, though this was not the entrance to the hotel section of the building, Jefferson Peters hurried to the door and unlocked and opened it, holding the lamp high, partly to illumine his smile of welcome and partly so that he could see the other.

He found himself looking up half a head higher than he would have looked for the average man. The stranger brushed past him into the room and, with a flirt of his heel, smashed the door shut. He was broad in proportion with his height, a man so large that, although he was hardly as old as the storekeeper, his bulk gave him great dignity. He was dressed in a cowpuncher's usual outfit, well-made boots covering his feet, while a great slicker, gleaming with rain, swept over the rest of his body and masked his arms, which seemed to be folded. The rain had soaked the brim of his sombrero until it drooped about his face—a wild and handsome face with sleek black mustaches and long black hair and black eyes, now glimmering at Jefferson Peters in the lamplight.

"Ah, Lord!" groaned the poor storekeeper as he looked upon the giant. "I'm done for!" And, stepping back, he threw up his arms as far as he could strain them above his head. "Don't shoot, Muldoon," he began to gasp out. "Don't shoot. I'll show you where the cash. . . ."

"Don't be a fool," said Muldoon. "I don't want your cash. You know me, then?"

"Of course I remember you, Bill," said the storekeeper, bringing down his hands by inches and keeping them in a quivering state of alertness to jerk them above his head at the first command. "I remember you at school, Bill, as well as I remember myself."

The other produced a hand from beneath the slicker and pushed back his mustaches until they glistened again and bared a smile which was half amusement and half pure contempt. There was a stir beneath the slicker and a faint sound. The smile of Muldoon vanished and, tossing the oilcloth over his shoulder, he revealed that he carried in his left arm a young infant. It put out both tiny fists and began blinking at the light. Muldoon thrust an immense forefinger in front of the child, and the finger was instantly clutched.

"Got a fine grip," asserted Bill Muldoon. He lifted his

head and grinned at Jeff. "Hangs on like a bulldog, hanged if he don't. He's going to have the grit, this kid."

"Most likely he will," said Jeff Peters flatteringly. "He sure will have it if he's got any of your blood in him, partner."

Muldoon received this communication with an undisguised sneer of scorn. "Peters," he said, "the kid'll be yapping in a minute or two more. And I got to be away before that happens. Listen to me! You remember two years back when you come down one morning and found the lock on your door busted?"

"I remember."

"That was laid to me. The fools! If I'd busted the lock, wouldn't I have gutted the store, no matter if the sheriff was in town that night? Sure I would. Matter of fact, the boys started to raid the store, but I recollected you at the school and the way you used to help me at arithmetic. Figures never done no good with me, anyhow. I say, I remembered you all at once and I decided that the gang could get along without ruining you."

"That was mighty good of you, Muldoon. It sure was!" said Jeff, his voice shaking under his effort to seem cordial. He did not believe a word of it, but it might mean death if he seemed to disagree.

"Well," said Muldoon, "you might say I done you that good turn looking to the future for a time when maybe I'd have my back against the wall and would need a friend."

"Nobody would ever say that," said Jeff Peters, forcing a noiseless laugh. "What could I do for a gent like you, I want to know?"

"More than you ever thought of doing," said Muldoon. "Look at this here."

He moved his hand from the grip of the child and doubled it into an immense fist. Instantly the baby balled its own pudgy fists and struck at the hovering threat. Bill Muldoon chuckled softly at the sight.

"All nerve and fire," he declared, "that's what little Jerry is made of. Now step up and take a closer look at him!"

The Black Muldoon

"He's sure a buster," said Jeff, bending a little as though on rusted joints.

"Does he look like any other Muldoon you ever seen or heard tell of?" went on the big man.

"Why, come to think of it, he's got the same sort of look around the head."

Muldoon broke into hearty but controlled laughter. "There ain't any chance of the women folks coming down here, is there?" he asked, breaking off his laughter and frowning.

"I dunno . . . no, I hope not!" said Jeff Peters, turning deadly pale. "Leastwise, they wouldn't tell nobody that they'd seen you here, Bill."

Muldoon cursed in a heavy whisper, as though a sudden rage half stifled him. "You little fool, Peters," he said when he could speak. "D'you think that I'd harm womenfolk? Man, ain't you got no sense?"

Jeff Peters was paralyzed by the dread of what his mistake might now bring forth. He could not speak.

"I ask you to look again!" he said. "D'you ever hear of a Muldoon that didn't have black hair and black eyes?"

"I disrecollect," said Peters, choking. "I dunno that I ever have, now that you mention it."

"Lord," groaned the giant, "what a man to have the bringing up of a Muldoon! But look again. Ain't them eyes as blue as the sky in the evening, I ask you? Or blue as a lake in the mountains?"

"They sure are."

"Jeff," said the other suddenly, with such a change of voice that Jeff Peters for the first time had the courage to look up into the eyes of his guest, "old man . . . he's the son of Mary Conrad, that was my wife."

"That girl with the yaller hair that lived over to Coffeytown? I ain't heard that you married. . . ."

"Nobody else ain't heard. And she died giving birth to Jerry, and so we can't prove to 'em, now, how happy we'da been. I got the marriage certificate, though, and nailed it to the door of the church in Coffeytown. Then I stole Jerry, and I come away."

He began to breathe very heavily and walked up and down the room with a rapid and irregular step. Jeff Peters turned his head to glance after the outlaw, and he dared not speak. He winced away when Muldoon paused before him.

"Jeff, when I come riding through the night, I got to thinking that what kills the Muldoons is the knowing that they're Muldoons. There ain't been a one of 'em for nigh onto fifty years, now . . . not a single one of the menfolk of the Muldoons . . . that have died peaceable in bed like a man should. They've gone with their boots on, speaking by and large, and they've gone down hell raising. But I ask you man to man, Jeff, is it the blood that does it, or ain't it just that they know they're Muldoons? And when they walk out with other gents, they're watched all the time like they were snakes about to strike! Yes, sir. When I was a little kid in the school, you remember how the whole tribe of the Saunders boys jumped you that day, and how I come running to help you? And, just because I was a Muldoon, not one of the Saunders tribe would stand to me. They all turned and run. Well, when a man grows up, feeling all the time that he's stronger than other men, the time is sure to come when he can take what he wants by might. D'you understand the drift of this, Jeff?"

"It's all clear, Bill."

"It does me a pile of good to hear you talk up like that, Jeff. Well, when I come riding through the night, I say with the wind in my face, and poor Mary . . . Lord bless her . . . lying dead behind me . . . and looking down on me out of heaven, if there is a heaven, d'you see? When I come through the night thinking to myself, Jeff, what I done was to say that Jerry must change his name and live his life never dreaming that he's a Muldoon. Could that be done? It didn't look none too easy to work. And then I asked myself who would take the upbringing of him? Who would want to do a kindness to a black Muldoon? I says that to myself, and then I recollected your face, Jeff. I remembered some good turns that I'd done you in

18

school, and I remembered some good turns I'd done you
since . . . like the night when I kept the gang from clean-
ing up on your store . . . d'you see!"

Jeff Peters tried to speak. His throat was so dry that he
could not utter a sound and only nodded.

"And so I've come to you, Jeff . . . and now that I'm
here, tell me what you'll do?"

Still Jeff could not speak. Was he asked to raise a Muldoon? He hardly knew what was asked.

"Will you raise him as your own son, and tell nobody
in the world where you got him, more'n that you found
him on your steps?"

"Bill. . . ."

"And here's something that would go along with him."

He tossed a thick bundle of bills into the hands of Jeff
Peters. The glance of Peters, falling, clung upon the de-
nomination of the outer bill . . . fifty dollars on that slip
of paper, and so many other slips beneath.

"That whole roll . . . I dunno how much there is in it
. . . if you swear to me that you'll raise him and not ever
tell a soul who is his father!"

"Kate . . . ," began Jeff Peters.

"Not even your wife. She's a good woman, but there
ain't no woman good enough to hear the secrets of a
black Muldoon and keep 'em."

"Give me the boy," said Jeff Peters. "And, so help me
heaven, I'll try to raise him like my own boy, by the name
of Jerry Peters."

"And if it should come out that a story was to go about
saying what his real name was, d'you know what I'd do,
Peters?"

"But it'll never come out!"

"If it did, Jeff, I'd ask no questions, but I'd come gun-
ning straight for you. D'you understand?"

"I understand, Bill."

"Then take Jerry."

The soft, warm bundle was placed in the arms of the
storekeeper.

"Now swear, Jeff!"

"I swear, Bill!"

"May the money do you a pile of good," said the big man with a peculiar smile. That smile vanished as he leaned and looked closely into the face of the strangely cheerful and silent infant. "And may Jerry see little of me? Between now and the day I bump off, hang me if I don't hope, for Mary's sake, that he never lays them blue eyes on me."

He turned and strode out of the room. The instant the door was closed, the storekeeper, devoured with anxiety, placed the child on the desk. There he rolled unheeded, scattering the precious papers over which Jefferson Peters had been working so patiently.

With his hands free, the latter hurriedly opened the roll of bills which the outlaw had given to him. The wrapper bill, as he had seen before, was a wrinkled fifty . . . but the bills within were simply a sheaf of one-dollar notes. Even in so great a crisis of his life, the black Muldoon had been a rascal. The poor little storekeeper raised his despairing hands to the heavens. Here was an added mouth in the nest. And, besides, what earthly explanation could he offer to Kate?

Chapter Two
Blood Will Tell

Eight years showed Jefferson Peters at exactly the same poundage, with exactly the same puckered and wistful brows. His hair had grown a little gray. His cheeks were a trifle more lean and wrinkled, but otherwise his face was the same. His back was somewhat bowed, now, but on the whole he seemed no nearer the breaking point than ever. For he was one of those men who anticipate the worst, always. And therefore, when the worst came, it was never a shock. It was impossible for him greatly to succeed, because he never dared greatly hope; but, for the same reasons, more or less, he could not possibly be a complete failure. For eight years he had carried the burdens of a wife, his twin boys, and that Jerry Muldoon who had been left to him, and who passed in the eyes of the world as an adopted son calling himself Jerry Peters. He was never given cause to doubt that his parentage was other than that of the two husky youngsters who played with him every day. So far no one in the village of Custis had taken upon himself to tell Jerry of his mysterious origin.

It was recess at the school, and Kate and Jefferson Peters sat by the teacher's desk. She was the proper mate for her spouse. Her square and placid brow as yet showed no sign of a wrinkle. For his wasting form she made amends in a steadily increasing amplitude of the waistline. She was not yet exactly ponderous, but neither could she be termed active. She carried with her one remaining quality from her girlhood spent on a ranch, and that was a straight and piercing glance which, on occasion, thrust her husband through to the soul and made that soul tremble. But, though she understood her power, be it said in her favor that she rarely abused it. She exercised her strength not more than once a year, as a sort of secret holiday pleasure.

But she had no reticence about abashing the school teacher. The latter was newly out of normal school, a mere child, eager as a hawk and keen as a whip, but rather painfully conscious of her youth as a handicap placed between her and the accomplishment of great ambitions. And school teaching was to Elsie Dennis a great ambition accomplished. Three generations of drudgery lay in the immediate past of Elsie. If instinct is an inherited thing, all of Elsie's desires should have turned in the direction of scrubbing floors or, at most, cooking in ranch grub wagons. Instead, she had risen by force of detestation of all she found around her and had turned to a future of higher education. Had Elsie been equipped with a pretty face, her way would have been far easier.

As it was, Elsie's round, serious countenance was set on the end of a long, scrawny neck, along which the unfleshed tendons played in and out whenever she moved her head. Weak eyes, outworn by the labors of prodigious reading, blinked feebly behind the great lenses of her glasses. Her skin was sallow. Her forehead was wrinkled with the anguish of mental labor. Her bony hand was tremulous and cold. Her figure was chiefly a matter of lines running straight up and down.

In spite of appearance, Elsie Dennis had a soul of fire. She could speak of an example of arithmetic or a lesson in geography with a flaming enthusiasm which shortened the breath of her pupils. She felt her inward fires quenched, well nigh, by the presence of Mrs. Jeff Peters. That lady, knowing nothing of books, had fortified herself with a high disdain. As a matter of fact, she was afraid to praise the gaunt school teacher because she feared that an expression of praise would be for the wrong thing and thereby expose her ignorance. But she knew, as many wiser persons have also learned, that it is easy to damn with criticism and appear intelligent.

"As for Harry and Jack," said Elsie Dennis, "I don't know which is the better." She was answering one of Mrs. Peters's very direct questions. "Harry is slower, but then, he works harder. Jack is much quicker, but he is a little lazy. . . ."

"Miss Dennis!" cried Mrs. Peters. "I dunno how you can talk about Jack being quicker! Anybody that's ever seen the two of 'em around horses. . . ."

She stopped, breathless with indignation.

"I've no doubt," said Elsie Dennis in her most gentle voice, "that Jack may be more apt with horses, but with books . . . you see, it isn't exactly the same with books and with horses. They're so different."

Mrs. Peters sat back with a superior sniff intended to indicate that no matter what the teacher said, she had her doubts about it.

"Well," said Mr. Peters, reverting to the immediate cause of their call at the school, "we want to know what can be done to bring up their standing. There ain't any natural reason, so far as I can see, why my boys shouldn't be right up with the leaders in their class."

"If they got the right sort of teaching," appended his better half.

Elsie Dennis confined her answer to the father. Somehow, it was always thrice as easy to talk to a man.

"The reason they don't lead . . . oh, it would be hard for any boy really to lead so long as Jerry Peters is in his class." Her eyes shone as she spoke. She threw back her head with a fine little outburst of enthusiasm, which, for the instant, made her actually pretty. "Oh, what a boy he is," she cried softly. "Sometimes he stares at me so hard when I'm talking or reading to the class that I think the words are being printed on his brain."

She looked down to the parents. She found that their faces were utterly blank and cold. It was Elsie's first term at the little school. She had not yet learned that Jerry was only an adopted child. And poor Elsie, bewildered, stared at the two in amazement. She knew that parental likes and dislikes are often hard to understand, but how any human beings could prefer such children as Jack and Harry to that restless flame of a boy, Jerry Peters—that was indeed beyond her!

"But with a great deal of special care," she concluded lamely, "I think that Harry and Jack may be brought up in time. They've improved a lot over their last year's record already."

"If Jerry has been favored so much," said Mrs. Peters, fixing upon poor Elsie Dennis her frostiest glance, "it's no wonder that little Harry and Jack are backward. Children can't be expected to get on when they're neglected, Miss Dennis."

Elsie Dennis crimsoned. Her lips trembled.

"And as for even comparing Jack, for quickness, with Harry," said the mother, "why. . . ."

She made an eloquent pause. Her spouse bit his lip and, stirring in his chair, cast anxious glances from one to the other. He foresaw a storm, and he almost equally dreaded the lightning cuts of Kate when they were directed at the head of another. He never knew when a random bolt would strike him.

"Dear little Jerry," went on Mrs. Peters, "is such a mischief . . . but, if you put up with that. . . ."

She paused again, sternly.

"I try to keep discipline," said Elsie Dennis. "Jerry is high-spirited . . . that is all."

Her color was gone now. Her fighting instinct was aroused. Another side fling at Jerry would bring fire from her.

Here they were interrupted by a shrill clamor in the school yard, followed by utter silence, and then the scurry of many running feet converging to a point. One keen voice pierced the air: "Fight!" And Elsie and her two visitors ran to the door of the school.

They were in time to see the slender form of Jerry bristling up to another boy of far greater bulk. The other youngsters of the school were scampering to form a circle, the boys pressing to the center, the girls at the outer rim on tiptoe, terrified and delighted.

"William!" cried poor Elsie Dennis. "Don't you dare to strike Jerry Peters! William, do you hear me?"

As well call to a thundering storm. At that instant big William smote in hearty earnest at the fire-red head of Jerry with such effect that Jerry tumbled head over heels in the dust, and there was a shout to witness the fall. Prominent among the rejoicers were Harry and Jack Peters, who saw many a downfall of their own now about to be requited with a vengeance.

But Jerry had come to his feet as by magic and, before William could follow his first advantage, he was assailed by a hail of fists. The air was thick with the showering blows. William, smiting in roundabout fashion, with eyes closed, struck nothing but utter emptiness, and all the time those hard, stinging little fists were cracking against his face. A trickle of red began to pour down from his nose. Both eyes and his mouth puffed. And then, retreating and raising a hand to his face, the fingers came away stained with gore.

The sight completely unmanned him. A loud yell of terror issued from his lusty throat. Turning on his heel, he fled for safety.

He would have gained it, perhaps, had there not been that circle of witnesses. But they impeded his course and, before he had taken half a dozen steps, there was a red-headed fury upon his back. Down he went with a final shriek of mortal anguish and fear.

Elsie Dennis and Peters, in the meantime, had hurried down from the front door of the school. All this part of the brief fight they had seen to the point when stout William crashed to the ground and now, as they went forward, the shrill shout of the onlookers turned to a cry of dismay in which the voices of the older boys predominated.

What Jefferson Peters, brushing his way through the tangle, found was William lying flat on his back and making faint gurgling sounds, while the hands of Jerry were buried deeply in his throat. William was far gone. His eyes were wide and popping out, his face was purple, his mouth was distended as he gasped in vain for air which would not come, and the older boys, in alarm, were trying to tug the conqueror away from his victim. But he clung like a leech.

It required the entire force of Peters to tear Jerry away, and then it was to divert the force of the attack to himself. There was a wild and mighty flailing of little fists at him. At length, dismayed, he brushed them away and captured the warrior.

But by this time the passion of Jerry had broken into outright grief. Suddenly, he began to weep. He pointed with mingled rage and disdain at the prostrate and gasping form of William.

"He said," gasped out Jerry, "that I haven't any father or mother, and that I just happened along and you found me, Dad. And I . . . I'll kill him unless he takes it back!"

"Jefferson Peters!" called his wife. "I hope you'll thrash that young man within an inch of his life. Look at the condition of William Jones! Why, in another ten seconds there would have been a tragedy. Why. . . ."

She was speechless. The real nearness of the catastrophe stopped her usual flow of words. But her husband had picked up Jerry and carried him to a little distance, and now he put him down with a suddenness which seemed to come from his weakness. His face was gray, and he was trembling.

"Mother," he said to Kate, "I guess this ain't the time for a thrashing. There'll have to be a talking first. Or maybe it's best not to talk, even. Blood will out. It ain't poor Jerry's fault. Blood will out!" He took Jerry by the hand, silencing the clamor of Mrs. Peters with a single gesture. "I'll take this matter in hand," he declared. "Let me manage it. Miss Dennis, we'll take Jerry out and home for the day."

They left the poor school teacher pale and trembling with concern for her favorite. She followed them to the corner of the yard, saying over and over: "Something went wrong. We all have our outbursts. Oh, Mister Peters, you won't be too hard on him?"

Jerry cast a wan and unhappy look after Elsie Dennis as they departed, but he said not a word and walked stiff and straight down the street ahead of his foster parents.

"And now, Jefferson Peters," whispered his wife sternly, "I'd like to know about the real father and the real mother of that boy! How come you been telling me for eight years that you didn't know?"

"Kate," said her husband, "you got to take my plain word for it. If you learn who his father was, it'll scare you plumb to death. And . . . I wish to heaven that somebody besides me could tell him that you and me ain't his real father and his real mother."

Chapter Three
Jerry Makes a Promise

The best way to make a secret delectable is to surround it with terrors if it is revealed. The one room we are forbidden is the one we truly desire to enter. And so it was with Mrs. Peters.

Yet fifteen years more passed, and the question which devoured her soul was never answered. Sometimes, to be sure, there came to her a poisonous doubt that Jefferson Peters himself might be the father of the boy. But that doubt never endured long. She knew that her husband was not a good actor; the fear with which he referred to the true parent of Jerry could not have been assumed. Therefore, during the fifteen years, she held her council.

In fact, the knowledge that her husband had guarded a great secret all this length of time had established her respect for him upon a foundation of rock. Hitherto, she had felt rather contemptuous. But thereafter she came to believe that, no matter how weak he was in appearance, there was a mysterious strength about him which was worthy of respect.

Moreover, of late Jerry had proved to be far from a bad investment. Jack and Harry had grown into fine young range riders no better and no worse than a thousand others. But Jerry was different. He was a man in ten thousand.

Ever since that day of the fight the character of Jerry had changed. He had become more sober, more quiet. Even at the age of eight he had seemed to understand that the mystery of his parentage would prove a weight hereafter. The world at large saw in him, at the age of

The Black Muldoon

twenty-three, a mighty-limbed young Samson with a clear blue eye and hair like blowing flame. It saw in him a bulwark of the community, a strength and support for Custis. No longer would they be unrepresented at steer-roping and mustang-riding exhibitions. In fact, they were turning to Jerry in the confident expectation that he would put them on the map.

Yet this universal esteem and all the prowess of his six feet two of strong muscle and bone had not served to turn the head of the young giant. Mere flattery could not affect him since that day when his foster father had told him that his real father and mother were unknown. For since that time an undercurrent of melancholy had been established in his nature. It had made him more quiet. It had tamed him, so to speak, and it had given him an air of command which was felt and admitted among young fellows of his own age.

In the meantime, he had developed habits of thrift from which the Peters family profited hugely. A venture at prospecting in his eighteenth year had given him a partnership in a mine which he turned over to Jefferson Peters, and that partnership had become a handsome business. In reality, it was the source of Jefferson's prosperity in his later life, though he carefully concealed from Jerry all knowledge of the handsome dimensions of the gift. For he and Mrs. Peters had decided at once that it would not do to allow Jerry to conceive that he had repaid all the years of care which had been given to him by a single stroke. And, by concealing the size of the donation from him, they continued to incur benefits. They became a prominent family in the town of Custis simply for the reason that Jerry brought home with him a good portion of the distinguished visitors.

What ambitious legislator could pass through the town of Custis without looking up that brilliant youngster who had won a second at the national horse-breaking contest in his twentieth year, and who had won a first on two successive years thereafter? What sheriff or federal marshal could come nearby without dropping in on so deft a marksman? Those whom Jerry met, the rest of the Peters family met likewise, with the result that they were in what Mrs. Peters, more than the rest, felt to be true social clover.

As for the immediate future of Jerry, he had only to choose one of a dozen openings. He could go into lumber or cows or mining; or he could play politics or start any one of a number of careers. For men of established position had their eyes upon him. To enlist the youth would, they felt, be guaranteeing their own futures. Honesty, strength, patience—what more could be asked?

When they put these questions to Jefferson Peters, the worthy storekeeper would nod and keep his own council. But all those years he had been waiting—for fifteen mortal years he had been unable to forget the picture of William, flat on his back, and the small fists of Jerry in the very act of throttling the other. That had been an indubitable outbreak of the bad blood of the black Muldoon, he had felt. And he had been waiting for another outburst, only wondering how the lightning would strike. If a child of eight, in a passion, had come so close to murder, what would this hard-handed giant do? And should he, in the meantime, risk the wrath of the black Muldoon in order to warn the boy of the bad blood that was in him?

He put off what might have seemed to others a duty, and the result was that he was out of town when the first great blow fell. A man on an outworn mustang, with a crimson-stained rag tied around his head and a shirt encrusted with red, spurred into town with tidings that the black Muldoon had just swept down with his gang upon New Custis, higher in the mountains, and blown up the safe in the store. It was the first time in twenty-three years that the famous outlaw had come near Custis and, while other districts in the mountains had suffered, the little town had come to feel that it lived a charmed life. But now that the blow had fallen on their neighbors, the men of Custis rallied gallantly for a counterattack.

The news reached Jerry in the house of Lou Donnell.

The Black Muldoon

As a matter of fact, most of his spare moments were spent in the house of Donnell. The Donnells were newcomers. They had not been in Custis more than half a dozen years and, though they were of rather better social position than any one else in Custis, Jerry was the first to secure an intimate relationship with them. He secured it by dragging young Mark Donnell out of the lake when the youngster was sinking with a cramp in the bitter chill of the snow water. After that, as a matter of course, the doors to the big Donnell house were open to Jerry night and day. The reason that he darkened them so often had little to do with Mark. Mark was a fine fellow, but his chief virtue was that he had a sister. There was a singular mystery attached to Louise Donnell, and that was that any girl with so much poise and inherent dignity as she should have had her musical name shortened to "Lou." But it had happened early in her life, and she would carry the nickname to the grave.

She was an Irish beauty, was Lou. That is to say, she had blue-black, lustrous hair which slunk low over a broad forehead. And under the black brows there were deep blue eyes. But the naming of color contrasts never paints the whole picture, and only an artist familiar with paints and their making can even faintly conceive the effect of black and blue and white and delicate pink in the face of Lou Donnell.

What is so hard to describe with words was easy to grasp at one effort of the eyes. At least Jerry had found it easy. Even six years before, when he carried Mark Donnell home on that fateful day, the sight of Lou as she ran with a cry to her brother had been a sweet and soul-thrilling shock. For six years he had been unable to disentangle from his memory the fair young face and the grief-stricken voice. A hundred times he had wakened from his sleep in the middle of the night, so keen had been the joy and sorrow of his dream of her. What wonder that he haunted the Donnell house.

And what did the Donnells think of him? Plainly, they considered him merely a boyish friend. They did not take him seriously for the simple reason that the pretty face of Lou had made them visualize a throne for her—millions or a title or some such roseate future was planned for the treading of her feet, and that penniless young Jerry could ever draw her from the great road to fortune never came into their minds.

The swirl of horsemen stormed to a stop at the verandah of the Donnell house. And from the shade beside Lou arose Jerry.

"Jerry!" they cried. "The black Muldoon . . . Bill Muldoon . . . he's raided New Custis!"

Jerry turned pale with joy. "That's a yarn somebody's been spinning," he said. "They're always talking about a Muldoon every time there's anything goes wrong!"

"I tell you," shouted one of the dusty riders, "that Oscar Little seen him with his own eyes. He's in Custis now, Oscar is. And he's got two bullets out of Muldoon's gun inside of him! And the sheriff sent us extra special to get you. He said you'd want to come, Jerry. And . . . don't turn us down, Jerry! We sure need you!"

"Muldoon himself!" said Jerry, and he tingled to the tips of his long fingers with an exquisite foretaste of pleasure.

The girl was turned in her chair. Leaning sidewise she read his face with a swift and faultless accuracy, as women can. She saw him white with pleasure. She saw him literally trembling with delight. She came out of her chair and caught his hands.

"Jerry," she whispered. "Jerry."

She was even oblivious of all the others, yet a country girl is the most self-conscious creature under the arch of heaven.

"I'll be back tomorrow," he was saying to her.

But she clung to him, and the clinging was wonderfully strange and sweet to Jerry. It had always seemed to him, before, that she spoke to him from a great height, a great distance. Now she had stepped from an eternity of distance and was close to him in flesh and spirit. He looked at her in amazement. Her eyes were filled with moisture.

The Black Muldoon

Her face was turned up to him in human entreaty. For the first time he noticed that she was really quite small. At least she was not above an average height, and she seemed small beside his bulk.

"Jerry, if you go, there's bad luck in it. Believe me!"

"It's the hot weather, Lou," he answered. "You're nervous, that's all. But it's pretty fine of you to be nervous on my account. I sure appreciate it."

"But I mean it, Jerry. It's more than nervousness, it's a premonition. Besides, Jerry, I think this man-hunting fever you have is horrible!"

"You've never said so before."

"I've never dared to think that you'd take my thoughts seriously. But today I'm going to chance it. Today, Jerry, you've got to listen and believe me."

"Lou, it draws me wonderfully hard. But they're all waiting." His voice became a whisper. "They're all waiting and watching us, Lou!"

"Do you think that I care what they see? Oh, Jerry, if you would only see half of what they can see, how happy I should be."

"What do you mean, Lou?"

"I mean that if anything should happen to you I'd never be happy again."

"Lou!"

"Hush, Jerry . . . but . . . I mean it. Oh, how ashamed I am to tell you. But I've got to keep you from going."

"Lou, after this one time. . . ."

"That's a promise you'd be sure to break. Don't make it!"

"It's a promise I'd be sure to keep. Lou, on my word of honor, after this one chase I'll never ride again with the rest of 'em when they take a man trail. But this is a black Muldoon . . . this is Bill Muldoon himself! Don't you see that I'd be shamed if I didn't go, just when I may be of use . . . ?"

Suddenly she turned and fled into the house. Just inside the screen door she paused, but she did not turn

33

again, and he knew it was because she would not show her weeping face.

He turned to the waiting group of riders. Every man had a faint smile of concern and envy at the corners of his lips. It is the concern of all men, whether young or old, when a beautiful girl gives her heart away. Those smiles of understanding went out as Jerry sprang down from the porch and leaped into the saddle of his horse. In a close cluster, shouting with triumph now that they had Achilles in their midst, they raced off down the road.

Chapter Four
Black Muldoon at Bay

It was the old trail after a black Muldoon. As always, they had taken to the ways leading to the rocky crests of the mountains. Above timber line the Muldoons seemed at home.

Also, they were always sure to be equipped with exactly the right sort of horses for traveling across the dangerous land where no trees grow. What their ponies lacked in speed over the level, they more than made up in ability to get about among the slippery rocks and crags of the summits. The men out of old Custis gained rapidly enough so long as they had tolerably even ground for the running of their horses but, when they got off the easy trails of the lower hills and entered into the precarious ways of the loftier mountains, they began to lose again. And when they came to the timber line, Sheriff Tom Smythe, old and reliable trailer that he was, gave up the battle.

"There they go yonder," he said after he had gathered his men into a knot. "I know where they go almost as well as if I seen 'em with the eye. They're cutting around the side of the mountain, in between Custis Mountain and Mount Black. They know doggone well that before night there'll be a storm busting across the pass and, if we foller them, they get through dead easy, and we'll get caught right in the pass. And that wind would blow the life right out of us, eh?"

The others agreed. It seemed to Jerry that for some time past they had been willing and even eager to quit the trail. Far to the north and west, a thin rift of storm clouds had been growing steadily. The prospect of being caught for a night above timber line in a wild storm was not alluring to the sheriff and his men.

"The way I figure it," suggested Jerry mildly, "is that what a Muldoon can stand the rest of us can stand, whether it's above timber line or by the seashore!"

"That's the way you figure it, son," said the sheriff, and he adjusted his bandanna around his bronzed and sharply wrinkled neck. "That's the way you figure, but when you're a mite older maybe you'll figure different again. I been following the Muldoons, off and on, about thirty year. And I ought to know their ways, pretty near, by this time."

It occurred to Jerry to suggest that thirty years of failure were fairly conclusive proof that the worthy sheriff did not know the ways of the Muldoons, but Jerry was enough of a diplomat to understand that such a challenge would destroy the favorable attitude of the sheriff and gain no desirable end.

But when the sheriff continued to say that he intended to make a detour, cross the mountains at Ball Pass, and then skirt up and down at timber line or just below, on the chance of meeting the black Muldoon and his gang as the latter went through to the farther side, the patience of Jerry gave out. He gritted his teeth in silence. When the sheriff actually turned to the side to start the detour, Jerry announced that, since the outright pursuit of the desperadoes had stopped, he intended to leave the party. It was in vain that the sheriff stormed and threatened that he would never again include Jerry in a posse. It was in vain that all of his fellows in the party of horsemen pleaded with him to stay. He was adamant, and at length they wound down the mountainside, growling and scowling at one another. Jerry remained behind.

He knew that he had dealt his prestige a heavy blow by this desertion, but the stupidity of the sheriff's conduct had angered him, and he decided that he would make the most of a lone hand. Had he not promised beautiful Lou Donnell that he would never again ride into the perils of

The Black Muldoon

a man hunt? What he could do single-handed against five desperate fighters and known villains such as Muldoon and his four companions did not enter into the calculations of Jerry. He only knew that he must get within striking range of the five, and after that he would let circumstances direct his own course of action.

But as to crossing with the sheriff to the far side of the mountains, that, of course, was absurd. There was just as great a chance that Muldoon would not cross the mountains at all but, having ridden to an upper height he would watch through powerful binoculars while the sheriff and his followers rode down the wrong way, and then he would double out like a fox from his lair and return by the same way he had come, to carry ruin into some mountain village. But if he did double back in that manner he would stumble against one obstacle—Jerry, with ready guns in his hands.

He got off his mustang and led the animal to the shade of a tree. There he threw the reins and rolled a cigarette, knowing, like every good range rider, that there is nothing like tobacco to clear the head and make the brain function smoothly. While he inhaled the first draft of the smoke deeply, he looked down toward the lower hills out of which they had labored this day. They were masked in a gathering haze of heat waves. He seemed to be looking into a vast well, in the bottom of which appeared dim forms of smaller mountains. Above him rose the barren sweep of the region over the timber line, with the timber line itself swerving in and out among the hillsides like the edge of dark water. An unseen bird swooped above him, singing out of the wind as it passed. Jerry raised his head to try and mark the minstrel, and he saw, with that upward glance, a file of horsemen twisting around a boulder on the side of Custis Mountain high above him.

He clamped his binoculars to his eyes. First rode a big man who had sweeping gray mustaches. That must be the black Muldoon just as he had been described when he plunged on his horse through the streets of New Custis with a revolver poised in either hand, guiding his horse with the pressure of his knees. Behind him was a flicker of red. That was Lefty, no doubt, who had been remarked in a red shirt. And behind came three more, winding into view one by one as they rounded the boulder, then dropping out of sight again at once.

The heart of Jerry bounded. There they came—there came five men, the capture of any one of whom meant fame to the captor. Evidently they had watched from the security of the mountainside, and hardly had they seen the sheriff lead his men to the side than they started their descent. It was plain that they were familiar from of old with the workings of the mind of the worthy sheriff.

It was hardly too late to summon back the sheriff and his men. Indeed, they could not be more than two or three miles away. But the noise which would summon them would also warn Muldoon and his followers back to safety. Jerry gripped his rifle at the balance and set his teeth.

High rocks near the tree sheltered both him and his horse from any but the most particular observation. The minutes spun out. The sun came hot and steady upon him. It seemed to press down on him with an actual and burning weight, as mountain suns will do. Perspiration streamed down his face. What if some of it ran into his eyes at the last instant? How many cool fighters had been ruined by such accidents as these? Perhaps all killers of men, in the end, were beaten by such chances as these. But his own coolness was gone. The thought of the black Muldoon shook him as the wind shakes a dead leaf.

Another idea came to him. Would he possess the cruelty, even if he had the nerve, to shoot upon the five men from ambush? That would be murder which the law sanctioned, but it was murder no less.

The long interval drew toward an end. He heard the clink of a rock under the iron-shod hoof of a horse, and then the leader of the procession drew into sight, the black Muldoon, to be sure, exactly as he had been described, a great body of a man, seen near at hand, active and powerful in spite of his middle age. He came with his hat pushed back on his head. His rifle was carried at a balance across the pommel of his saddle, and all his manner was one of easy command and self-assurance. And, to be sure, had he ever once been cornered? Had he ever once been beaten?

Jerry tossed the butt of his own gun into the hollow of his shoulder and drew a bead. Instantly, as the sights lined up with the head of the outlaw, his hand steadied to a rocklike firmness. Bill Muldoon was no better than a dead man. Moreover, Jerry had now a practical assurance that his nerve would by no means fail him in a pinch. All that he needed to do was to press with his trigger finger and the notorious long rider would have been no more.

But the instant he was sure of one he desired a greater prey. There were five men there. If he started shooting from covert, the swift action of the repeater would probably account for them all while the marksman remained uninjured. But could he shoot from covert? It was the sense that such a thing would be no better than murder that had kept him from shooting the black Muldoon. Now all five horses were in plain view, with their heads nodding in a ragged rhythm.

Jerry leaped sidewise from his shelter among the rocks, and he fired an opening shot above the head of the last rider of the five.

That was his last concession to sportsmanship. Even as he fired into the air, he was dropping prone along the ground so that he would offer a smaller target to his enemies. They had seized their guns, one and all, and reined their horses wildly back. But before they had located him, his rifle spoke again and the last man of the five slumped in the saddle. It exploded again and knocked the fourth rider, a tall, lean man cleanly out of his saddle.

At the same time the three leaders found the marksman and sent a volley crashing at him, but surprise had affected their control and every shot flew high while Jerry, in quick succession, cool as ice and wondering at his coolness, sent two more bullets home and saw the third rider and the second, he of the red shirt, struck headlong from their saddles. All the time used in the firing of those four shots had been hardly a breathing space.

There was a new explanation of why Jerry had lived to complete that string of four, however. He saw the first man, the great Muldoon himself, swing the rifle around his head with a tremendous curse and hurl it at the head of Jerry, then whip out a revolver and leap from his saddle at the same instant. The larger weapon had clogged in some manner so that it was no longer useful. He should have opened fire with the smaller from the saddle, but a blind rage seemed to have overcome him, and he plunged in the end to combat hand to hand.

Jerry had risen to meet him. In the flurry of that wild rush they both fired and missed, and then they fell into each others straining arms, dropped the revolvers, and strove for wrestling grips.

Well was it for Jerry then that he had youth on his side. The black Muldoon was within a year or two of fifty, but he carried his sinewy bulk with the agility of a boy. Moreover, all the Herculean power of that great frame was used according to the methods of a trained wrestler. Opposed to that skill, Jerry had only a novice's conception of the grips. But he had tireless strength, the grip of a coiling boa constrictor, and enough lifting force to have riven up a young oak by the roots.

Even so, he found himself caught, twisted and flung headlong onto the rocks. Only a catlike agility in whirling over and over and throwing himself to his feet in a single effort saved him.

He dodged the next rush of the big man and, avoiding the deadly pressure of those thick arms, crashed both fists against the head of the black Muldoon. This brought forth a terrifying roar from the giant. In he came again. Half a dozen pile-driver blows glanced uselessly from his lowered head. Again he caught Jerry and again Jerry went down, and this time in such a manner that he could not work loose.

He labored in the moments that followed as he had

The Black Muldoon

never labored before and would never labor again. Had the big man followed any single plan of attack he would have crushed Jerry infallibly in that assault, but he clung to no one plan. There was only a half-blind and consuming fury to dictate his courses. He no sooner did one thing than he saw another tempting opportunity. He quitted a grip which threatened to crack the ribs of Jerry in order to tear at his throat, and he left the throat hold for one by which he strove to crack the bone of Jerry's right arm.

But his hurrying ferocity defeated its own end. Grip after grip was changed, purposely, or else Jerry managed to writhe away from it, though the fingers of Muldoon tore his flesh like hot irons. Those terrible efforts, however, had taken the first flush of the older man's strength. Incomparably powerful though he was, his apogee of might endured only through one ecstasy of action. A hoarse and gasping breath warned Jerry that he had less to fear. With a great effort he managed to break loose and, when the black Muldoon charged again, a well-directed blow, whipped in with all of the younger man's strength, stopped Bill Muldoon in full career and sent him staggering back.

That was the turning point.

The moment big Muldoon's fighting impetus was gone, Jerry showed him the same mercy that a tiger shows to a wounded bull buffalo after a fierce battle in which both have bled. He would not at once close, for he still dreaded the bone-breaking power in the arms of the older man. But gliding around Muldoon, he slashed at him with terrible blows. Solid as was the bulk of Muldoon, it needed only that one of these blows lodge squarely on his chin to down him. And he, realizing this, held his head down, and glaring up from under bushy black eyebrows, he waited with a species of savage patience for a time when he might get his opponent at a new advantage.

But that time never came. A bone-crushing left hand drove against his ribs. He gasped and instinctively his head came up as he struck hard and short in return. The raising of that head was what Jerry had been waiting for.

41

At the same instant his big right fist, brown as a berry and hard as a rock, slugged the black Muldoon across the jaw, and dropped him with a grunt.

Yet such was the marvelous vitality of the man that before he had well struck the ground he was writhing to regain his feet once more.

But Jerry had had enough. He had met the huge outlaw with the latter's own weapons. He had beaten him hand to hand. Now that this was accomplished, he could not find it in his heart to beat the older man further with his fists. And it would have been brutally ludicrous to ask that heart of oak to surrender.

So, as the black Muldoon came staggering and half blind to his feet, Jerry scooped up his own fallen revolver and thrust it into the giant's pit.

"Stick up your hands," panted Jerry.

"Shoot and be damned to you," gasped Bill Muldoon, and as he spoke a crimson stream trickled across his lips and stained his gray mustaches. "Shoot, you prancing hound . . . you skunk . . . you yaller dancer! If you'd of stopped still for five seconds, I'd of smashed you like a bad egg!"

Jerry waited patiently. Words could not harm him. Even the working hands of the outlaw, hovering perilously near his throat, could really do him no injury while the cold nose of his Colt was shoved against the stomach of his foeman. Moreover, he knew that it was the first time in Muldoon's life that the latter had surrendered to any foe.

"Now that you've finished talking," said Jerry, "get them hands up!"

"I'll see you to the devil sideways, endways, or anyways you blame please," said the outlaw. "I've told you to shoot!"

"That was just your way of letting off steam," said Jerry. "Why, you murdering dog, d'you think I'll think twice before I blow you in two? You're worth as much to me or any man dead as you are alive. Get up them hands!"

The outward thrust of his jaw, and the admonitory jab

of the Colt, caused the other to sag as though his spirit were broken. His hands came halfway to his shoulders. Then his eyes rolled to the side.

"Lemme have a look to the boys," he breathed. "And then I'll get up my hands as high as ever you please. Will you lemme have a look to them?"

It was, in a way, a giving or parole and, though Jerry accepted it as such, he nonetheless kept his revolver in his hand all during the time when the leader was bending over his followers.

"I'll give you my word, if you want," said the black Muldoon.

"I want no promise from you," said the youth. "If you can get away from me, why, then you're well and welcome to get away."

Chapter Five
The Last of the Outlaw Gang

Muldoon went at a run first to the red-shirted man, scooped him up in his arms, and then lowered him with a breathless oath.

"Lefty's done!" he gasped out. "Lord a'mighty, after all of these days, Lefty's luck run out on him, and here's the end of him, and the end of the trails that him and me rode together."

That epitaph must suffice, perforce, for poor Lefty. The giant leader had hurried on to the next man and there he shouted with triumph as the latter opened his eyes and feebly asked for water. The third man lived also, but the fourth, whom Jerry had first aimed at, was shot cleanly through the head and had never known the end that struck him down. Big Bill Muldoon, nervous with haste, panting with the labors of his battle, and with his wounds dripping unheeded where the hard fists of Jerry had slashed the skin, picked up the third man, whom he called "Bud," and placed him beside the second, who had been previously addressed as "Hank." There, where he could listen to both and work over both to the best advantage, he labored first to quench their thirst from their own canteens and the canteens of those who would never again need water. Next he examined their wounds and jerked his terrible face around to speak to Jerry.

"They're about ready to pass out. Four shots to end four men the like of them! By heaven, I can't believe it even if

44

The Black Muldoon

I had seen it. No smooth-faced kid like you done that work."

He dropped upon his knees in the rocks before them.

"Boys," he said, "buck up. Get your chins off'n your chests. You're about to die."

The man named Hank lifted his lolling head, raised a tremulous hand, and smoothed back his long, tow-colored hair. His languid eyes turned from his leader to Jerry and back again. And then a faint light of satisfaction settled upon his face.

"It sort of appears to me, old-timer," he said to the black Muldoon, "it sort of appears to me that you ain't going to be terrible backward about following us down to the devil, after leading us most of the ways to him."

Bill Muldoon shrugged his shoulders at the thrust. But through the dirt and the red stains, Jerry saw that the face of the leader was flaming with shame.

"I done my best," said Muldoon. "But . . . but . . . I was beat by a gent, here, that took me at a disadvantage."

"You lie," said Bud, gasping forth the words. "You lie, Bill. I was enough alive to see that fight . . . and I seen my money's worth. The kid beat you fair and square."

The black Muldoon ground his teeth and all of his great bulk of a body shook with his passion.

"No matter about me," he said, "it's you boys that I'm thinking about now."

"And I'm thinking about you, chief," said Bud, "and how you used to say that nobody but a Muldoon could ever beat a Muldoon. Was that a lie?"

"If it'll make you happier, Bud, I'll call it a lie. But now, old son, you just start in thinking about what's lying ahead for you."

Bud sneered, but the muscles of his face had grown flaccid and the expression of defiant contempt changed to one of dismay on the instant. He reached out a fumbling hand which big Bill Muldoon received in his own.

"Steady, Bud," he said with amazing heartiness. "Steady, old-timer. It ain't more'n one twist, and then you go to sleep."

"I don't mind the pain," said Bud, a very feeble voice through his panting. "I don't mind the pain, but the kink in the mule's tail for me is that after I'm dead somebody else is going to ride the pinto. Come here, you fool hoss!"

It was a sturdy little brown mare with a great white patch on her side. She came to the voice of her master and shoved her nose under his chin with ears that quivered back and forth.

"You old fool!" gasped out Bud, passing an arm around her neck. "You old good-for-nothing, you! Lord, Bill, it sure is hard to leave a hoss like this in the middle of a trail."

"Bud," began the black Muldoon, and then stopped short, his voice choking. And Jerry looked upon them in utter amazement. "Bud," said the black Muldoon when he could at last speak, "I'll tell you what I'll do when you've gone along. I'll take the pinto and take the saddle off'n her and turn her loose to run wild. I'll send her back to the kind that she came from."

"Good old Bill," said Bud, his voice now weakened to a horrible whisper. "Good old Bill. I sure always knew that you'd be my friend in the last pinch. You won't sell her? You won't let no other gent take the saddle on her?"

"Nary a one, Bud."

Here Bud started up, raising himself by a terrible effort upon his elbow.

"But you ain't got the say no more. What about him?"

He pointed a shaking finger at Jerry, and the black Muldoon turned with a gesture to his captor, a gesture imploring him to tell a pleasant lie.

"I'll see that the hoss is turned out wild," said Jerry.

With a glance the black Muldoon thanked him. And Bud stretched out his hand. Jerry took it. It was limp. There was barely enough strength in the dying man to give one pressure to that handshake, and then he dropped back, dead. Muldoon closed his eyes, and no sooner was that duty done than he turned to the other victim of Jerry's rifle. With trembling hands Hank had managed to roll a ragged cigarette and had lighted it, though he had barely power to lift his hand to his lips. Not a murmur escaped him, though his pallor was more from the mortal anguish he endured than from the loss of blood.

"I took a look to Bud first," explained Muldoon as he went to Hank. "I done that because he was the weakest . . . he was the kid. I knew that he couldn't hold out so long as a ornery old critter like you, Hank!"

A faint smile of gratified vanity stirred the lips of Hank, though he banished it at once.

"Yep," he said, "you can't expect much out of a kid like Bud was. Still, take him by and large and he done noble, that kid done!"

Jerry looked again at the face of dead Bud and, by that second examination he saw, to his vast surprise, that Bud had really been only a youth in his twenties, a slender fellow no older than himself, though he was wrinkled and scarred by too much experience too soon acquired. And now he looked more closely at Hank himself and he began to see that the latter, veteran though he considered himself, could not have been more than a year or two older than poor Bud. Yet, with a half smile and a half sneer he regarded the body of his dead companion, raised a shaking hand to his lips, and blew forth another cloud of cigarette smoke. But now death was coming upon him fast. His face was gray. His lips were a light purple. The smile was a stiff caricature of mirth upon his lips.

"Sure he done noble," said Bill Muldoon heartily. "He done his best. He wasn't quite the man that you are, Hank, but for a kid he done pretty well. But if all the gents that rode with me had been as hard as you, Hank, we never would of run into a mess like this one. I ain't forgetting that you was for going straight on to the far side of the mountain, or else turning back and laying an ambush for the whole posse. I ain't forgetting what you advised, Hank."

The dying face of the boy brightened.

"Well," he said, "if we'd of done that we'd of blowed

about twenty fools clean to inferno instead of getting stopped, all of us, by one blamed tenderfoot . . . one. . . ."

He rolled his eyes up to Jerry. Inexpressible disdain curled his lip.

"That's done and over with," said Muldoon hastily. "And you can take this for a comfort for you, son . . . that the fight that finished you is the fight that finished the last of the Muldoons! Don't that please you, Hank?"

"Well, Bill, could a Muldoon of fought for you any better than I fought?"

"No, sir, they couldn't," said the black Muldoon heartily. "You've come second to none."

"Though Lefty wouldn't of heard to that!"

"Lefty was a fathead. He didn't know nothing that was really worth knowing, I guess."

"I'd like to of had him hear you say that," said Hank.

"He was about to hear it, too," said Muldoon. "I was going to let you handle the Murphysville job all by yourself and have Lefty working under you."

"The devil you were, Bill," whispered the dying marauder.

"I sure mean it!"

"Well . . . I wished I might of lived to do that job."

"You can do a better job than that, partner. You can make your mind easy. You can give me any messages that you want to send down to the folks in your old home town."

"The devil with the old home town," said Hank. "I got no use for it or the folks that're in it."

"What about your old dad? He'd like it if he thought you remembered him when you come along towards the end."

"Would he? Well, it was little that he ever done for me, and why should I want to be thinking about him now? Let him go!"

"And there's your girl, Flossie. What about her?"

The face of Hank contorted with savage pain and anger.

The Black Muldoon

"She'll marry that Perkins gent, and to the devil with her and him both. I hope that ranch raises more salt than cows for 'em. Yep, she'll marry him and forget about me, quick enough."

A touch of hardness came into the eyes of Bill Muldoon, but he only said: "That's a way folks have. They forget us plumb easy. But now we've got our medicine and I guess we ain't the ones to whine about it. We'll take what's coming to us, Hank, eh?"

"Sure. You ain't heard me whining!"

"Tell me what I can do to make you easy, Hank? Want me to roll you another cigarette?"

"No! Can't I roll my own? But . . . Bill . . . let's talk about the day we rode down and cleaned up Jerneytown."

"Ay, that was a day, Hank."

"D'you recollect the big fat barber coming to the door and throwing up his hands with a yell when he seen us?"

"I recollect him like I was seeing him now."

"I shot him plumb in the belly. My Lord, how it tickled me to see him flop. What come of him, Bill?"

"He got well, by and by."

"The devil he did! But I remember that I was using some old shells that day. They didn't do much good. And d'you remember how the cashier . . . ?"

"Steady, Hank!"

The robber's head had fallen suddenly back with a strangling sound. But now he dragged his head up again and stared at Bill Muldoon with tortured eyes.

"I'm steady enough. And . . . I got my boots on, Bill, eh?"

"You sure have, Hank. And you're the last man of the gang, too."

"Well," breathed Hank, "when you come to think of it, I am the last. And . . . and . . . Bill . . . ?"

The leader leaned low over the other.

"Bill," came the raucous whisper.

"Well, Hank? I'm right here listening."

"I guess I ain't showed any white feather, eh?"

"Nary a bit. You show the white feather? I should say not!"

"Well, then, I guess there ain't nothing more for me to wish for. Bill, s'long. . . ."

All his limbs contorted wildly. He started up to his knees. But to the very last he kept the cry of agony between his locked teeth. And when he slumped sidewise into the arms of Bill Muldoon he was dead.

Chapter Six
A Proposition Turned Down

Bill Muldoon closed the eyes of Hank as he had done those of Bud, and then arose, stretched himself, and rolled a cigarette.

"Well," he said, "so that's done."

His forehead gleamed with perspiration and, when he had lighted the cigarette, he drew great breaths of smoke down to the bottom of his lungs. He had the appearance of one who had just completed some strenuous physical labor.

"Hank was a fool," commented Muldoon to Jerry. "But he was a brave fool, what?"

"He was," said Jerry.

"About the pinto . . . I guess you ain't aiming to really turn the mare loose?"

"You heard me tell him that I would."

"That was to make him pass out plumb peaceable, I supposed."

"He was dying," said Jerry, "and I promised. There ain't no good comes out of a broken promise that's been give to a dying man."

"Suppose I was to take that saddle off of the pinto now?"

"Go ahead."

Haltingly, as though he expected a counter command at any moment, the outlaw stripped the saddle from it and sent it flying away with a stroke of the bridle reins.

That done, the big man turned with a grin of satisfaction to Jerry.

"I guess you didn't know what hoss that was?" he said.

"I know all about that hoss," said Jerry, smiling. "That's the hoss that Sheriff Galbraith and his posse followed for a whole week down south and couldn't catch up to."

"And you turned him loose?" said Bill Muldoon in great wonder. Suddenly he shrugged his shoulders as though determined to pay no further attention to that which mystified him. "Now, partner, suppose that we get down to business."

"It's about time," said Jerry. "We got a long ride ahead of us."

"A long ride?"

Jerry smiled at the apparent misunderstanding.

"We're going to get back to Custis as fast as we can move," he said.

Bill Muldoon shook his head.

"I been thinking from the first that you didn't know me."

"I know you well enough, Muldoon!"

"Ay, but I'm Bill Muldoon."

"What of that?"

"Why, look here, friend, I could see how a whole gang might want to take in Bill Muldoon if they ever caught up with him, but I'm dead sure that no one man, not one as intelligent as you, partner, would ever do it."

"No?" said Jerry noncommittally.

"I say no, and the reason why is that there's too much money tied up in the taking of me."

"Money?"

"Such a pile of it, partner, that it'll make your mouth water when I tell you how much you'll get on the split."

"Half to each of us?"

"That's right! Now, what would you think I had laid up, stranger?"

"Not much, I should think," said Jerry.

"No? You ain't followed my doings, then?"

"I have."

The Black Muldoon

"And you figure I ain't made enough to do any saving?"

"I figure that a gent that would rob and murder when he ain't starving for the lack of money is a hound too bad to live," said Jerry fiercely.

The big man winced suddenly, as though he had been shaken by a blow. And, staring fixedly at Jerry, he passed the tip of his tongue over his bruised lips.

"It's the second time," he said slowly, "that you've laid murder at my door, friend."

"Look here, Muldoon," said Jerry, "if I stay here and listen to you, it don't mean that I'm believing what you say. Not a bit of it! I'm simply listening to a pile of interesting lies. But the facts about you, Muldoon, why, you're a fool if you suppose that every man-jack in the mountains don't know 'em."

"I'm talking about murder," said Bill Muldoon. "First I ask you, write down the name of one man I've murdered?"

"Well, there's the Gaffney boys."

"They came man hunting on my trail down in the Pecos country. I met 'em both at the same time. They got the drop on me. They had me helpless. I surrendered and put my hands over my head, but them dirty yaller hounds shot me down and, while I was lying on the ground, I got out my Colt and finished the two of 'em . . . but I was laid up three months getting over the wounds that they give me."

Jerry gaped. It was impossible to doubt the veracity of this tale. How many almost mortal wounds had cut and broken the body of this giant during his life of pillage?

"And Jud Harlan?" he asked. "I suppose that he got the drop on you?"

"He didn't," said Muldoon calmly. "There was a gentleman, was Jud Harlan. When they made him sheriff, he just sat down and wrote out a nice, polite letter that he sent to some friends of mine, and he tells them to let me know that he's about to start out on my trail, and that when him and me sights each other we'd better start clawing for guns. And that's exactly what he done. We met up head on coming around a mountain. I beat Jud by the least mite of a second and filled him full of lead and he dropped down the mountain side and I even rode into the next town and told them where they'd find their sheriff. And when it come to building a monument for old Jud Harlan, didn't I send in one thousand dollars in cold cash?"

Again Jerry was stunned. But how much of all this was the truth? Or had the black Muldoon been fiercely maligned all of his life?

"You mean to stand up there and be telling me," he said at last, "that you never killed a man just for the sake of killing him?"

"So help me, partner," said the black Muldoon, "that's just what I do mean to tell you. And if I could get them that started the lying, I'd break their backs. Why, friend, yarns like that are the things that a lot of yaller-livered cowards make up about a man they're plumb afraid to face. They ain't the stories that an honest-to-God man like you should be believing."

The flattery warmed the very soul of Jerry.

"Matter of fact," said Bill Muldoon, "what you and me are going to do is to be partners. I been waiting all my life to find just one good man instead of a gang of bums. And you're the man for me, I can see that."

"Am I?" said Jerry, reserving his judgment.

"Sure. You had the nerve to jump out from behind the rocks and take a sporting chance when you could of killed us all dead easy from there. And then when I rushed you, instead of drilling me easy with your rifle, like you sure could of done, you met me at my own game and . . . and"—he spoke through his teeth—"and you had the luck of it."

He could not speak again for an instant, but then he continued more cheerfully: "The trouble with a gang is that so many men can always be followed and always be found. But a gent like you and a gent like me . . . why, we'd be as good as twenty such as them that lie back yonder."

The Black Muldoon

What a consummate hypocrite the man, thought Jerry, but he said not a word. Silence more than once had undone a clever man, and it seemed about to undo the black Muldoon, likewise. He was led on.

"To begin with," he said, "we'd split up fifty thousand dollars that I've got laid away and you could take your share and go have a party."

"And what sort of a story should I be telling folks about how you got away?"

"They'd never know that you ever took me. But you'd be down yonder with twenty-five thousand dollars to spend, and more coming to follow it up with. And with you working free at that end of the line, we could pull off some jobs that would make the sheriffs of six states go plumb raving crazy!"

"Bill," said Jerry, "it's no good. If you had two hundred and fifty thousand dollars to offer, it wouldn't be near enough. If you had two million and a half, it still wouldn't be half enough. What I say is, to the devil with you and your lies! You go to town with me and hang for what you've done. Money can't buy back them that you've killed, and money can't save you."

The outlaw answered nothing. Instead, he spent a moment looking fixedly at Jerry and then asked abruptly: "What's your name?"

"Jerry."

"Jerry is your name? You maybe ain't out of Custis?"

"I am."

The black Muldoon, to the utter astonishment of Jerry, turned white. Then he stepped closer.

"Keep away," said Jerry, "or I'll knock you down with a gun barrel."

Bill Muldoon, upon whose lips eloquent words had been trembling, halted and closed his mouth.

After a moment he said: "Well, let's be starting on!"

But there was something new in his manner. There was something repressed and hidden which alarmed Jerry. It was as though the great outlaw had suddenly discovered that his captor was helpless in the hollow of his hand.

They mounted, took the other three horses in lead, and started on down the mountain trail with big Bill Muldoon riding in the lead, his feet and hands free although his weapons had been taken from him.

Behind rode Jerry, his revolver in its holster. And behind him came the horses of the dead men.

Chapter Seven
The Conquering Hero

It so happened that the worthy sheriff, having changed his mind about continuing to the far side of the range and there awaiting the possible coming of the brigand and his followers, had decided that the best possible move would be to ride straight back to Custis and there organize a larger and more efficiently mounted band, at the same time getting in touch, through telegraph, with other communities in the mountains so that they could move in harmony and throw a cordon around the probable location of the outlaws. He had ridden into Custis, therefore, with his hot and dusty followers behind him, and the townsfolk had merely sighed in their disappointment. Because, of course, there had been no real expectation that this expedition would end in the destruction of the outlaws. That would have been too much distinction to fall to the posse of any one small mountain town. No, the sheriff was not considered any the less worthy because of this failure and, indeed, when the townspeople looked up to the lofty tops of Custis Mountain and Mount Black and saw that the summits were wrapped above timber line in black storm clouds, the sheriff was simply praised for a discretion which had kept him from exposing his posse to such hard weather.

It was in the midst of such feeling that a strange murmur ran down the single street of Custis, a dumb rumor which began because a half-naked urchin had galloped bareback into town with a report that he had seen, coming down the road—but no matter what he had seen. It was disbelieved, contorted. And the rumor suddenly took form that the terrible Muldoon, the black Muldoon himself, was about to rush upon the village with his desperate retainers and distribute death as he whirled through their midst. That rumor, in an instant, searched out every man in the village. It roused them. It put loaded guns in their hands. It made them mutter to one another: "By heaven, that Muldoon is going too far. This time we'll finish him unless he has a charmed life!"

The sheriff himself heard the story. He had just enough imagination to believe that it might be possibly true. And, gray with the shame that such an attack would bring to him, whether Muldoon fell in the attack or survived it, he got out his best rifle, looked to his revolver, and came out armed and stood at the door of his house, a conspicuous and rather absurd figure, if any one had had an eye for humor at that moment.

Into this picture, then, came a procession, and what a procession it was! First of all came the terrible figure of the black Muldoon, looking no less mighty in reality than he had been painted in a thousand stories of him. For thirty years he had carried terror through the mountains. Two generations had told their stories of him. And it was wonderful that he should seem as heroic in fact as in fancy.

Behind him came the conqueror, the late treasonable defector from the sheriff's posse—behind him came flame-haired, blue-eyed Jerry, sitting erect and jaunty on his horse, keeping his joy under restraint as befits men in great hours. And behind him came three horses. Did that mean that besides the great leader three of his followers had been struck down, and by the hand of that one youth? What triumph had David compared with this?

People started out into the street. Women who had been whispering together ran forth clutching one another, and they, in turn, saw the miracle. They saw young Jerry spring down from his horse and walk up to the sheriff. They saw him point to the prisoner. They saw the sheriff wring Jerry's hand—and then all was a joyous tumult which swerved and swirled around Jerry the foundling. Mrs. Jefferson Peters came and paraded where all the village could see her. And Elsie Dennis, who had been held to the teaching of that same school all of the last dusty, hopeless fifteen years, confined to it because her spirit was not hard enough or her face pretty enough to make her a way to greater places—poor Elsie Dennis came running out with her prematurely white head bare, and found Jerry, and cast her arms around the neck of her favorite and wept on his neck. But that was only one of many wild actions in Custis that day. For the town had awakened to the fact that it had a celebrity in its environs. No more talk of riding championships—here was a man made of that heroic clay out of which other noble forms had been molded in the history of the frontier. Here was material for the making of the youngest sheriff in the history of the West. Here was the man whose terrible name would keep all outlaws at a safe distance from Custis.

At the end of that day, Jerry sat at the table with his foster brothers and his foster mother. He said nothing at all about his exploit except to belittle it to cheer up Jack and Harry who were terribly downhearted at this latest feat. But all during the meal, no matter what words were spoken, they all had had but one thought in their minds until Jefferson Peters came home late, hungry and tired from a day of riding.

He had not heard. Oh, the joy of telling such news to one who had not heard even an inkling of it! With compressed lips and shining eyes they endured during the dinner he ate until he was midway in his second piece of pie, his third cup of coffee. And then they exploded.

"Dad, have you heard?"

"Heard what?" he said petulantly. "What the devil is eating you folks? You sit there and stare at me like I could be eaten!"

"It's Jerry!" chanted three voices. Even Harry and Jack had lost their jealousy in a wave of family pride.

"What have you been doing, Jerry? You been out buying another hoss, maybe?"

"No, he got three hosses for nothing!"

"What the devil are you talking about?"

"Jefferson, how can you use such language?"

"I can't help it, dear. It sure riles me to hear such talk. Three hosses for nothing! What d'you mean by it, Jerry?"

But Jerry, pink with happiness and dumb with modesty, was rolling a cigarette and waiting until the ordeal should be completed. He could not answer.

Mrs. Jefferson rose from her chair. She stood like one presiding at a meeting held to defend the rights of downtrodden American womanhood.

"It just means, Jeff, that we got a hero with us."

"Mother!" exclaimed Jerry in faint protestation.

"I mean it! That word ain't none too good for you, Jerry boy. Jefferson, today this Jerry of ours went on the trail of the Muldoon gang that raided New Custis."

Jefferson Peters arose from his chair likewise. He rose as one being dragged up by the hair by an invisible hand. He said nothing. His joyous anticipation had very much the look of speechless horror.

"Go on," he urged. "Hurry!"

"The sheriff missed Muldoon and Muldoon's four desperadoes," went on Mrs. Jefferson Peters, "but our boy would not follow him when he turned back. Instead, he stayed behind by himself. By himself! I'm covered with gooseflesh at the thought of it. One boy against five terrible men! But there he stayed. And the first thing you know, down they come, and out stands Jerry, and down they go, one and all."

"No!" shouted Jefferson Peters.

That cry might have been taken for incredulous joy. At least, Mrs. Peters so took it.

"He killed four men and captured the black Muldoon in a hand-to-hand fight and didn't get a scratch himself, and now Bill Muldoon is down in the jail in this very town. And six men are guarding him day and night."

She crowded the cream of all her tidings into that one

great sentence. The effect upon her spouse was strange indeed. He rushed around the table at her with both hands raised high in the air as though to beat back the words he had heard and destroy the truth which they represented.

"Don't say it," he said. "For God's sake, don't say it!"

"Don't say what?" shrilled his wife. "Are you gone crazy, Jefferson Peters? Ain't you got any realization of what our Jerry has done for us, and Custis, and the whole of the mountains? Why, there ain't a paper in the country that won't have a long story of this."

"You fool!" gasped out Jefferson Peters. "Heaven help us . . . poor Jerry."

Jerry came suddenly before him.

"Now tell me what's up," he said. "Have I done something that's wrong?"

"Done something that's wrong?" echoed the store-keeper. "Why, ain't it liable that they'll hang him?"

"Hang black Muldoon? Of course they will, unless he's lynched first."

"They'll hang him," wailed Peters, "and the hand that puts the rope around his neck will be yours!"

"Doesn't he deserve hanging?" asked Jerry sternly. "Is he a friend of yours? Was it by his help that you managed to buy the store when . . . ?"

"No, no!" stammered Peters.

"Then what do you mean by such talk?" asked his wife, advancing into the fray.

"Nothing!"

"Don't talk like a fool, Jefferson. You sure got some meaning in what you've been saying."

"I don't mean nothing. I don't want to talk to you. I got to be alone . . . and heaven guide me to what's right."

The great body of Jerry blocked his path. The great hand of Jerry held his shoulder.

"I've got to know," he said simply.

A sudden fury came over Jefferson Peters, one of those passions with which weak men, relying on their known weakness, bully men far stronger. He tore himself away from the detaining hand. He shook his fist in the face of big Jerry.

"You blockhead," he shouted. "You big blockhead! When they hang Bill Muldoon, they're hanging your father, and you're his murderer!"

Jerry staggered back to the door and leaned against it, weak, still blocking the escape of Peters from the room.

"Say it over again," he gasped out. "Say it slow so's I can understand. You ain't meaning that black Muldoon . . . but I knew it when I faced him. I knew it when I couldn't send the slug home into him. Oh, heaven help the two of us now."

Chapter Eight
The Red Muldoon

He left those four tortured and shocked faces and stumbled out into the night. The air struck suddenly cool and sweet against his eyes. He realized that they had been on fire—that his whole body was on fire. He was in a fever of anxiety, grief, terror.

He was a Muldoon then. He was one of those terrible man destroyers, the Muldoons! He looked back over the years of his young life. When we are young, we are not fitted to criticize ourselves. And it seemed to Jerry that there were scores of facts which fitted in with what had now been told him. There were those fierce and sudden passions of his childhood, for instance. There was that murderous attack on William in the school yard on the never-to-be-forgotten day when he had been first told that he was really not the son of Jefferson Peters. And there were other occasions when his temper had risen to a white heat. It had been bitterly hard to control himself on those occasions. The explanation was simple in the light of what he had learned on this day. It was simply the instinct of the Muldoons urging him to strike.

A black Muldoon! They would call him the *red* Muldoon, after this. Jerry Muldoon. The very ring of the name dwelt in his mind with sinister implications. It would be a good name to give a murderer.

"Jerry Muldoon, stand up!"

Those were the words the judge would speak. The last scene flittered before his eyes. He blotted it out with a savage oath and, running to the barn, he saddled his strongest horse and led it out. There the sound of softly rustling skirts met him in the darkness.

"Jerry, Jerry, Jerry!" he heard the voice of Mrs. Peters calling to him.

And to think that he had once thought of this woman as his mother.

She found him. She threw her arms around him. "Jerry, where are you going?"

"I'm going to see the girl I love."

"Ah, that'll be Louise Donnell."

"Yes."

"Jerry, don't go to see her tonight. Wait until word has been sent to her. Wait until she's been prepared."

"I'm not ashamed of being a Muldoon," he said bitterly. "I ain't a bit ashamed of it. Maybe they've been bad men, mostly, but that don't keep them from once in a while turning out an honest man, too. Am I right?"

"Of course you're right. But people won't stop to think . . . at first. There's been a horror around that name . . . Muldoon! Maybe there's a lot that's untrue blamed onto them. I don't doubt that there is. But they've got the bad name for them things, just the same. D'you see how it is, Jerry?"

"Oh, I see, right enough, but listen to me. Bill Muldoon . . . my father . . . he's a real man. When I captured him today, he found out my name and that I come from Custis and he knew right then that I was his son. And right then he could've got clean off by telling me. But he wouldn't tell. He decided that he'd take his medicine."

"Ay, that was a terrible thing to do . . . and it was a fine thing to do, Jerry dear."

"Only a big man could've done it. He gave me to you and Jefferson Peters in the hopes that I would be raised honest. And he wouldn't spoil my life to save his own, if the name of Muldoon might spoil a man's life."

"But you ain't going to take that name, Jerry? You're still going to call yourself Jerry Peters, ain't you?"

"Lord a'mighty, d'you think that I'm ashamed of my father's name? I'm not. I'm wild proud of it!"

The Black Muldoon

"Jerry!" Her voice was a wail of sorrow. "Jerry, oh, Jerry boy, you're going to leave us!"

"You'll not be sorrowing very long for that," said Jerry bitterly. "I guess I've been a weight on you all these years. Keeping back Harry and Jack."

She clung to him.

"Don't be saying that, Jerry." She began to weep. "Oh, Jerry, I ain't been as good to you as maybe I might have been. I've been real hard and mean to you more'n once. But when I seen you leaning against the door after Jefferson told you . . . when I seen you so sick and weak from what the words had done to you, but what the fear of bullets couldn't do . . . when I seen you standing there, Jerry dear, all at once I loved you as though you were my own child, like Harry and Jack. Can you understand, dear boy? No, no man would understand . . . but oh, Jerry, if you're leaving us now, it's my flesh and blood that I'm losing. Stay with us and let me show you that I love you, Jerry."

"I'm coming back, I guess," he said. "Only I'm going to see Lou Donnell first. . . ."

"Won't you listen to me, Jerry?"

"Of course. But that can't change me. Besides, it's a good test. If she cares a single flip for me, this won't make any difference."

"Now you speak only because you're bitter, dear."

"No, it's the straight truth. If she was to marry me, would she be marrying my father? What difference does it make, what my father may have done?"

"The Donnells are terrible proud folks, Jerry."

"And so are the Muldoons!" said Jerry.

"Are you going to talk to her like that?"

"Why not? I'm not ashamed of my blood."

"But the shock of what she hears . . . remember how the shock of it hurt you, Jerry."

"It didn't hurt me. It only staggered me sort of, for a minute. But after that. . . ."

"If you go tonight, you'll lose her. Trust a woman's judgment that far, Jerry."

"If I lose her, I'll never come back to win her again."

She only sighed.

"Good bye, and God bless you for coming out to talk," he said. "I'll never forget it, not in a hundred years."

He took her in his arms, kissed her, and then took the saddle and drove away at a smashing gallop over the gravel road. And on through the night he never let the horse slacken until he had passed Custis and the big, blunt outlines of the house of the Donnells rose before him. Then he stopped, threw the reins, and approached the verandah more slowly.

Luck favored him here, at least. He came through the darkness just in time to see Lou's father disappear into the house, leaving Lou herself alone on the verandah. When he walked up the steps, she rose with a cry of surprise.

"Jerry, Jerry! You've remembered us even on your great day." Then, as he came closer and into a keener light, she cried: "Jerry, there's something wrong! What is it?"

Clothes, says the resolute Westerner in his overalls and flannel shirt, clothes make no difference in man or woman. But the feeling of Jerry, at that moment, belied that maxim. For Lou Donnell was dressed all in white. Neither was it the sort of white that Jerry was used to. It was not crisp and flouncy, and apt to blow askew in the wind. Instead, it was of shimmering silk and, when Lou moved, she was accompanied by a hushing whisper of the fabric. And this dress was made, also, in a manner which suggested money—much money. Jerry knew that although he saw no details. But the clothes of Lou Donnell removed her to a strange distance. He could not talk to her with assurance. He became stiff and wretchedly self-conscious.

"I've come over to tell you some queer news," he said.

"But I know all about the fight," said the girl. "Dad was in Custis today and he heard everything and he's come home chanting your praises. He says that you're a hero, Jerry, and everyone else in the house agrees. Dad went to the jail with the sheriff and heard that terrible black

Muldoon tell everything. And even Muldoon didn't take away any of your credit."

The head of Jerry fell. But how could she know how cruel a cut she was giving him?

"D'you know why he wouldn't take any credit away from me?" said Jerry.

"You mustn't be mysterious about it."

"I'm going to be as plain as day. Lou, he's my father!"

He had expected a cry of fear and sorrow. Instead, she merely folded her hands and blinked at him.

"You know," he explained, "that I'm not really the son of Jefferson Peters. And tonight, when he heard what I'd done today, Jeff broke out and told the whole story, how my father had come to the store at midnight, twenty-three years ago, and made Jeff swear never to tell whose son I was, and how Jeff took the oath and promised to raise me up to be an honest man . . . and . . . Lou, are you going to take it like that?"

For she was backing toward the door. As she stepped back the light struck across her face and he saw that she was deathly white. He followed her a pace, but she threw up her hand.

"Don't," she whispered.

"You're afraid," said Jerry. "I might of known it. You're afraid."

"Dad!" screamed the girl.

Footfalls rushed toward them from the interior of the house. Donnell and Mark Donnell plunged out through the front door. And there they confronted Jerry and Lou with wonder.

"What on earth, Lou?" began her father.

She clung to him. "Send him away!" she cried. "Send him away!"

"What the devil have you been doing?" asked Donnell.

"He . . . he's the son of black Muldoon!"

"Good Lord, Jerry, what nonsense have you been telling her?"

"The truth. The flat truth!" said Jerry Muldoon.

"Good Lord," breathed Donnell.

And Mark Donnell's hand instinctively sought his gun. Jerry waited to see no more. He turned, walked slowly down the steps, and threw himself again into the saddle.

Behind him, as the roar of the hoofs began, came the voice of Donnell calling his name, but Jerry paid no heed and spurred harder on the road back to Custis.

Chapter Nine
An Amusing Yarn

There was no one at the sheriff's home. He was a minor figure on this great day. And when Jerry came in, the man of the law rose and greeted him with a restrained enthusiasm. In fact, he was sick of the name of Jerry and the sight of him was very far from welcome.

"Sheriff," said Jerry seriously, as he shook hands, "I've come around to have a little private talk with you."

"Step in here, then."

They went into the sheriff's little office.

"Sheriff," said Jerry, "I thought that I'd drop around and tell you that I don't see this business the way the rest of 'em do! Not by a long shot. I know that I had no right to leave the posse. . . ."

"It wasn't a particular good example for discipline, I guess," said the sheriff mildly. "Not even if it turned out good."

"Sure," said Jerry, "the luck just broke on my side. And I'm here to tell you that I know if you'd been there, you would've done the job just as well as I did it."

"I dunno about that, but. . . ."

"Matter of fact," said Jerry, "it's too easy for folks to forget how much you've done."

"Well, I can't say but that there's some truth in that, Jerry. And I'm sure glad to see that your head ain't turned by what the boys been saying to you all today."

"Well," said Jerry, "I just wanted you to know what I felt, and that the next time you picked a posse, I'd be plumb glad to ride with you, Sheriff, and I wouldn't be breaking any orders the way I did today."

Max Brand

The sheriff's heart was touched. He wrung the hand of Jerry.

"You're a good lad. Jerry," he said. "I always knowed it, but now I'm dead certain."

By tomorrow, thought Jerry bitterly, he'll know—and the whole town will know. Then what will they be saying about the son of black Muldoon? But he controlled his emotions so that he could continue to smile. Indeed, that he was able to act his part so easily in this interview was proof to him that the blood of Muldoon was indeed showing in him.

"But there was another thing," he went on, wondering how it was that the Peters family had kept from spreading the news during the evening, "and the other thing was that when Muldoon tried to buy me off. . . ."

"He tried to do that? The hound!"

"D'you blame him?" said Jerry. "But anyway, he offered me big money. He said that twenty-five thousand. . . ."

"Twenty-five thousand!" exclaimed the sheriff.

"Apiece," said Jerry. "That much for him and that much for me. That was what he offered."

"Good Lord," murmured the sheriff. "But then, there's no reason why he shouldn't have that much cached away. He's stole that much ten times over."

"But it sure seems too bad to me," went on Jerry, "that all that money should go to waste."

"It sure is a shame," said the sheriff, "but there ain't nothing that can be done, I guess."

"I'm not so sure."

"What's in your mind, Jerry?"

"Suppose I go talk to him in the jail? Suppose I talk to him all alone. Suppose that while I'm there I make a bargain with him . . . if he'll tell me where the money is cached, I'll guarantee to get him loose?"

The sheriff bowed his head to conceal a sneer which twisted his lips. Such miserable bargaining was not at all to his taste but, if Jerry was willing to do the dirty work, he felt that he had no right to refuse.

"You go do the talking, son," he suggested.

The Black Muldoon

"But how'll I be able to talk to him alone?"

"You and me'll go down to the jail together. How does that suit you, old son? I'll send the others home and let you take over the guarding of the jail. After what you done today, I guess that there won't be none that kick at that idea."

So they started at once and went down the street to the little square, stone-walled building which served in Custis as a jail. It was simple and it was unpretentious, but from those massive walls no criminal had ever escaped. Such was the formidable record of the sheriff.

It was not difficult to dismiss the volunteer guards. Jerry was this day the most popular man in the town, and he could do very much as he pleased in all matters. He would have been allowed to guard a dozen black Muldoons single-handed had he so desired.

So they cleared out and the sheriff waved good-bye. Jerry was left alone with Bill Muldoon. The latter was lying on a cot in one of the two cells which filled most of the interior of the little building. He had put his hat over his face to shut out the light and so soundly was he sleeping that, even through all the loud talk that had greeted the arrival of Jerry, he still kept on snoring. Jerry walked to the bars and looked him over.

Lying prone, the outlaw seemed more huge than ever. In spite of Jerry's own size, he wondered how he could have stood for a moment before the assault of such a warrior.

"Muldoon!" he called.

The sleeper who had remained impervious to all other sounds responded instantly to the calling of his own name. He sat up, put the hat on his head, stood up, brushed back his mustaches, blinked his eyes, and on the instant was ready for whatever might come. Jerry could not but wonder at such prodigious self-control.

"So it's you, eh?" said Muldoon, advancing toward the bars and looking Jerry up and down. "You've dropped in to let me see what a great man you are, eh? Well, kid, you lay to this. It ain't you that beat me. It's the law. The law always wins. It's got loaded dice. And you . . . well, you just happened along at the right time and the law used you for its tool. That's all that you figure in on."

Jerry smiled. "That's all, eh?" he said.

"What else?" demanded the black Muldoon. "If I had a chance at you again, I'd smash you to bits, you young hound."

"Dad," said Jerry, very pale, "you could have that chance, I suppose."

"What?" said Muldoon, but his voice lowered quickly. "What did you call me?"

"Jefferson Peters has told me everything," said Jerry quietly. "And I've come to set you free."

"Jefferson Peters? Jefferson Peters?" echoed the bandit, as though he had never heard the name before.

"Yep, he's the man," said Jerry.

"And he told you . . . what?"

"How you came twenty-three years ago about midnight and made him take me in and promise to raise me like I was one of his sons."

The black Muldoon spread out his legs and hooked his thumbs into his belt. "So you're the brat, eh? You're the kid that I took to him that night?"

"I am," said Jerry.

"Well," said Muldoon, "Peters sure done a fine job in the raising of you. Might I be asking did he teach you how to shoot, besides?"

Jerry watched him, amazed. There was no fatherly pride, no gleam of joyous recognition in the face of Muldoon.

"And you called me Dad on account of me bringing you to Peters?" said Muldoon.

"Didn't you tell Peters that you were my father?" gasped out Jerry, as a flash of hope sprang into his breast.

"Tell Peters? Did I tell him that?" Suddenly the giant broke into tremendous laughter and smote his thigh flat-lings with his hand. "By God," he said, "I begin to remember chunks out of that night. And . . . it seems to me that I did tell the little storekeeper something like that."

"And it wasn't true?"

"No, you fool! Do you look like me? Nope, I picked you up out of a sheepherder's cabin. He was dead and his wife was dying. I watched her pass out and then I picked you up and brought you along for luck. That's all there was to it. I gave the storekeeper a yarn so's he would be kept amused. And there you are!"

Chapter Ten
The Head of a Family

But Jerry, startled though he was, kept a steady eye fixed upon the outlaw, and it seemed to him, as he did so, that the fellow could hardly meet his gaze but, turning away, stalked up and down the cell and now and again indulged in fits of heavy laughter.

"Listen to me," said Jerry suddenly, "if you can prove that you're my father, Bill Muldoon, you go free out of this jail. I've come here for that reason. I've got the keys turned over to me. I've got guns for two. I've got a hoss outside and I can get another hoss while we travel. Say the word, Bill, and you and me go on together and do what you was trying to buy and bribe me into doing this morning."

Bill Muldoon halted in his pacing, strode to the bars with a muttered word of triumph, and then stepped back once more with an oath.

"I'll see you to the devil, first," he said. "I'll see you to the devil before I call you any son of mine!"

But Jerry, watching very closely, saw that the face of the older man was shining with perspiration, and all of his great body was quivering and trembling as though with exhaustion. Suddenly Jerry unlocked the door to the cell and stepped in. Onto the bed of Muldoon he tossed a bunch of keys.

"There's what'll get you safely out of the jail," he said. "And here's a gun for you to start working with." As he spoke, he passed a Colt into the hand of the black Muldoon. "Muldoon," he said, "if you're not my father . . . if I'm only a stranger to you . . . the son of a sheepherder

74

that you never knew . . . why, Muldoon, what's to keep you from shooting your way out of this jail? Start going, for when you make a pass with your gun, I'll know certain sure that you are't any father of mine. Start up some action!"

Bill Muldoon, facing him in anguish, suddenly tossed the gun from him with a shudder.

"Jerry," he said, his voice changing to a peculiar moan, "the Lord is witness that I didn't ever want you to find out. And your mother that's watching somewheres . . . she'll sure put a curse on me for what I've done today."

Jerry Muldoon thrust his own weapon back into the holster. He leaned there by the iron bars only the fraction of a second. Then he stepped forward and held out his hand. At his touch the anguish melted wonderfully out of the eyes of the black Muldoon, to be replaced by a sort of childish marvel.

"Dad," said Jerry, "when I saw you up there on the roof of Custis Mountain, I must've known you. Something kept me from shooting when I had the bead drawn on you! It was something working in both of us, Dad, that kept us from doing a killing up yonder."

"Jerry," whispered the other.

"Ay, Dad?"

"D'ye mean it, Jerry? D'ye mean that you ain't hating me and despising me and wishing me dead?"

"Me? Why in heaven's name should I wish you dead?"

"Lad, I've busted my word to your mother. When she was a-dying with her heart plumb broken, I swore to her that I'd never let you know that a black Muldoon was your father! Because she knowed well enough that it might lead on to all kinds of bad luck in your life."

The arm of Jerry Muldoon passed around the wide shoulders of his father.

"There's only one thing worth thinking about," he said, "and that is that you and I have found each other. And after that the next thing in order is for us to get you out of this jail."

"So that the blame of it can come on you, Jerry?"

Max Brand

"D'you think I could ever hold up my head among folks if they didn't know that I'd done my best for my own father?"

"Jerry, I'm fighting hard to be honest and to do what's right by you, but how can I talk against you?"

"You can't, because it isn't natural or right. Dad, we're going to do what's right for both of us. D'you think that I'm ashamed of being a Muldoon? I'm not. I'm glad to find out that I am one. It makes me a pile stronger. It makes me a pile surer of myself. It . . . it's the biggest day in my life!"

He thought back to the girl he loved, and the terror in her face as she had heard his true name and denied him. And, in a fury, he repeated: "To the devil with them that hate the Muldoons! There've been black Muldoons before . . . but now I'll show them what a red Muldoon can do."

"Jerry. . . ."

"Only say you'll do what I want for tonight."

"I'll do that, Jerry . . . and God bless you, lad. When I heard your name up yonder on the mountain, and when you told me that you came out of Custis, right off I knew you, and right off I begun to think what we two could do if we was to start teaming it together . . . y'understand, Jerry?"

"There's nothing to keep me back," declared Jerry. "I've busted loose from everything that might hold, Dad."

"How come that? Jerry, is there a girl in it?"

"She got the horrors when she heard what my full name was," said Jerry. "She got the horrors and called for help. Well . . . she'll need no help to keep me away from her. Why should a Muldoon be ashamed? We've never backed down to no man that ever stepped and why don't we figure as well as the next with a girl? But I'm through, Dad . . . I'm plumb through with the whole job."

"Wait a minute," said the father, his fleshy brow corrugated with thought. "Just wait a minute, Jerry boy. How long have you been fond of her?"

"That doesn't count . . . about six years, maybe."

"Six years . . . and that doesn't count? Listen to me,

The Black Muldoon

Jerry. There was a time when I started to break loose from the old life. There was a time when I figured that one woman was worth more'n the whole rest of the world, Jerry. And so her and me got married and . . . so help me God . . . I fought to lead a clean and honest life. But it wasn't no use. I'd done too much before. Folks found me out and hunted me down. They drove me away from her. They broke up our home. But right up to the very end, Jerry, I've always figured that one happy year with her to be worth more'n all the rest of my life rolled into a lump. D'you hear? And you, lad, haven't made the break yet. You've been honest, so far. Maybe it'll be a hard thing for you to live down . . . but, after a time, folks'll see that you ain't following in my footsteps. They'll see that you're trying to be square all around . . . and then you've got a happy chance for a real life opening up to you. You understand, Jerry?"

"Dad," said the boy solemnly, "you're trying to hang yourself!"

"I'm an old man," said the black Muldoon. "I ain't fifty, but I've lived enough to fill five hundred years. And I'm ready to die . . . I deserve to die."

"It's no good," said Jerry. "Why . . . Dad . . . every word you speak simply makes me love you. Give you up? I'd go through anything for you!"

The father was silent for a long moment. At length he made a gesture of surrender.

"Go get the hosses, lad," he said. "Before morning we'll show them what two Muldoons can do! But first . . . before you go, Jerry, give me the picture of the girl."

"What girl?"

"Give me her picture, I say," roared the black Muldoon suddenly, and Jerry, in humble obedience, took out his wallet and gave him the treasured picture.

"Now get out and rustle the hosses," said the black Muldoon. "They's got to be a head in this family, and I reckon that I'm it!"

Chapter Eleven
With His Boots On

That last sentence seemed to Jerry to reveal more of the true nature of his father than everything that had been said before. And, passing slowly up the street, he sketched to himself the life that was before him, the constant alarm, the many dangers, the brutal companions, the more brutal adventures. There would be the first robbery, the first holdup, the first safe cracking, the first murder!

Yes, call it what they would, a battle of guns between one possessing his skill and an ordinary man was nothing better than a murder. Many a brave man in the West, Jerry knew, had accepted a challenge and fought a fight of which he knew, before the start, the inevitable outcome. But in such battles as these he loathed the thought of himself as the aggressor.

There would be ruthless raiding of houses in search of provisions. There would be the stealing of horses in the midst of pursuits. There would be stealthy night approaches and sudden flights. There would be the price laid upon his head as it was laid upon the head of his father. These were the thoughts which thronged in the unhappy brain of Jerry Muldoon as he went up the street of Custis, and wondering why God permitted such unhappiness in any man.

At the hitching rack in the front of the Peters house he saw a horse which he did not recognize as any of theirs. He paused to look more closely. There was something very familiar about the neat-limbed creature—he looked more closely still and his heart leaped, for it was the mare which Louise Donnell rode.

He circled hastily to the side of the house and then slipped up onto the side verandah, his blood turning cold as he realized that this was only the first of a thousand similar maneuvers which he must execute in his life as it now promised to stretch before him. The sound of voices came out to him through the opened window. Louise had just arrived. Mrs. Peters was busy making her welcome, and at the same time herding the Peters men out of the room. The door closed behind the last of them as Jerry reached the window and, looking in, he saw Lou drawing off her riding gloves and wringing them nervously.

"Missus Peters," she said, "I have to see Jerry!"

"You haven't seen him already?" asked Mrs. Peters.

"I . . . yes, but I must see him again . . . at once. Where can he be if he isn't here?"

"I can't say. He'll come back, I suppose, in a short time."

"Then . . . ?"

"Shall I give him a message?"

"Yes . . . no . . . but tell him that I came and that I'm very eager to see him at once and . . . but, oh, if he doesn't understand!"

"Louise, I think I know what he went to talk to you about this evening."

"He came to tell me that his father is the black Muldoon!"

"Yes."

"And at first it was a horror to me. I turned away from him . . . I . . . I . . . ."

"You either fainted or you called for help."

"I called for help. Dad came out. And then Jerry swore he was proud of being a Muldoon and he turned away with a face as black as thunder and went off into the night. The moment he was gone we all tried to call him back, but it was too late . . . and here I am, Missus Peters. And I must see him!"

"Does Mister Donnell know that you've come?"

"Yes. He sent me. He was the one who vowed that it made no difference. He said, too, that any man was a cur who was not proud of his father's blood, no matter what that father might have done and the rest of us agreed with him. I agreed, at least. What difference is it to me if Jerry's father is the black Muldoon? The black Muldoon is simply a man who was stronger than other men and has not been careful enough of his strength. Suppose my father grew up wild? Might he not have been just like the black Muldoon? At least, that's what I feel and why I have to find Jerry so that I can tell him."

Jerry stepped back from the window. He was almost too stunned with surprise and with anguish to keep from following the first wild impulse to rush into the room. But he ruled himself. His decision was not to be made here. It was made long before when he promised his father liberty. And what was a woman, no matter how he loved her, compared with the tie of blood between him and his father?

He staggered across the verandah, dropped to the ground beyond, and then made for the corral. Even in that anguished moment he made sure that the horse his father was to bestride was the best on the place. What matter whether or not that horse belonged to him? They could pay for that horse later out of Jerry's own money.

He chose a mighty gray gelding strong enough to drag a plow but surprisingly fast, likewise. That gelding he roped and saddled at the barn and then made a long detour back to the jail, cutting around behind the houses so that there should be a smaller chance of detecting him. He tethered the gelding beside his own horse and then, with a last agonized look down the street where the twinkling lights of the Peters store told that Lou Donnell was waiting for him, he entered the jail.

There was no black Muldoon waiting for him. The great outlaw had ridden his last ride, fought his last fight, cursed his last oath. He lay prone on his back in the middle of the floor with the Colt clasped in one hand and the left hand also relaxing from a bit of paper.

The Black Muldoon

And when Jerry examined the fingers he discovered that they had been gripped around the picture of Lou Donnell.

They buried the black Muldoon on the highest hill overlooking Custis and they heaped for him a great monument of rough stones. Sometimes, in the days that came, Jerry would say to his wife, "But Lou, how can we tell the children everything that my father did?"

"Are you yourself ashamed of him?" she would say.

"No," he would always answer.

"Then," said Lou, "tell them everything from the first. Half truths don't help. Because, you see, no matter how many crimes he committed during his life, he knew how to die like a brave man for the sake of others, and I think that death makes his whole life beautiful!"

There were others, and they were numerous, who did not agree with Lou. They held that the black Muldoon had been terrible and graceless to the very end, and they explained his death as an accident. But as for Jerry—as for the red Muldoon—if any had their doubts of his virtue, if any waited for the bad strain to show, at least they were afraid to speak up where other men could hear them talk.

YELLOW DOG

Perhaps no single year in Frederick Faust's literary career was as filled with remarkable fiction of all kinds as 1934. In *Argosy* several of his most important serials appeared in installments, including "The Red Pacer" which became *Red Devil of the Range* (Macaulay, 1934) and "Scourge of the Rio Grande" which became *Smuggler's Trail* (Harper, 1950). In Street & Smith's *Western Story Magazine* he published "The Gun Gift" which became *The Rancher's Revenge* (Dodd, Mead, 1934), "The Tough Tenderfoot" which became *Marbleface* (Dodd, Mead, 1939), and "Man of the West" which became *The Dude* (Dodd, Mead, 1940). The year 1934 also saw first publication of some of Faust's finest historical novels—serialization of *The Naked Blade* (Greystone Press, 1938) and *The Firebrand* (Harper, 1950). He contributed such memorable short stories as "The Sun Stood Still" in *The American Magazine*, "The Wedding Guest" in *Harper's Magazine* (arguably his finest short story and certainly one rife with profound symbolism), and "Beyond the Finish" in *Collier's*. His detective novels included *X—The Murderer* and *Cross Over Nine,* both serialized in *Detective Fiction Weekly*, as well as notable short crime stories for *Dime Detective*. Popular Publications agreed to buy 200,000 words by Max Brand in 1934 and a good part of this fiction consisted of the seven short novels featured that year in *Star Western*. It was hoped Max Brand's popularity would do for *Star Western* what it had done for *Western Story Magazine* a decade before. Three of these are unquestionably classics of the Western story: "Lawman's Heart" in the May issue, "Outcast Breed" in the October issue, and "Yellow Dog," which was retitled "Gunman's Bluff" when it appeared in the April issue.

Chapter One
The Heel of Achilles

Of what good is a ham-strung horse, or a blind dog, or a hawk with clipped wings? And when the right hand of a gunfighter has lost its cunning—the right hand, that almost thinking brain—freedom and hope are gone from the victim.

That was what Dr. Walter Lindus was thinking as he examined the big fellow who had come in half an hour before and asked, a little uneasily, for treatment. He sank his fingertips into the strands of muscle that sprang from the base of the man's neck and ran in broad elastic bands over the shoulder. At the point, just above the shoulder blades, where the muscles curved from back to front like the grip of a many-fingered hand, the doctor encountered the gristle scar-tissue and felt the flesh shrink from his grasp.

He looked hastily up into the brown face of his patient and saw that the smile persisted on the lips of this young man, but that the eyes had grown suddenly stern. The patient had stripped to the waist for the examination, and the pain had been sufficient to make his belly muscles pull in and the chest expand a little.

"How did you get this?" asked the doctor.

"Hunting accident," said the patient.

"Rifle bullet?"

"Yes."

"The other fellow was careless, eh?"

"Yes."

"Those things happen. I would have said, though, that

the other fellow had been careless with a forty-five caliber Colt. Eh?"

The youth said nothing. His calm blue eyes moved without meaning across the face of Doctor Lindus, then journeyed through the window and over the roofs of the houses of the town, through the shimmer of the heat-waves that made the mountains tremble in the distance.

Doctor Lindus ran exploring fingertips through the lower muscles of the arm. Even above the elbow they were firm; below it they twisted into a beautiful tangle of whipcord. Lindus stepped back. In addition to the scar in the right shoulder he saw a long white streak over the left ribs.

"Another hunting accident?" he asked, pointing.

"Had a fall from a pitching bronc and hit a rack," said the patient.

The doctor walked around his man. Across the left shoulder blade was a white zigzag, inches long. It was a very old wound.

"And this . . . another fall from a horse?" he asked, touching the place.

"I suppose so."

"Out of sight, out of mind, eh?" asked the doctor.

"That's it."

The doctor permitted himself to smile. He faced the man again.

"Mister Jones," he said, "does this right arm feel a bit numb?"

"Yes."

"Tingling, now and then, as though the muscles were asleep, eh?"

"Yes."

"Anything else you can say about it?"

"No. It's just the damned left-handed feeling that's come into it. I've got two left hands. And that's no good."

"Particularly for you, Mister Jones. I mean . . . for a fellow who runs into so many accidents?"

Mr. Jones said nothing.

From the beginning of the interview he had said little.

He seemed to be one who looked first and spoke afterward. Now his blue eyes turned almost gray with light as they thrust into the mind of Doctor Lindus.

"There's a big nerve up here," said the doctor. "It branches out here. That nerve has been injured."

"How long will that right hand be crippled?" asked Jones.

"I don't know," said Lindus slowly. He saw that he had struck a heavy blow, but the lips of Mr. Jones continued to smile. The shock appeared in his eyes, only.

"You don't know how long it will take to fix me up?"

"Sorry, my friend. I really can't tell."

"Perhaps you mean, Doctor, that I'll *never* get that arm back in shape?"

The doctor drew in a long and very soft breath. Out here on the range he was accustomed to handling big, powerful men, but he had never seen a specimen like this youth, strong as a bull but looking swift as a deer, also. The head was magnificent, too, and it was carried with the lofty pride of an unbeaten champion. That was why the doctor had to pause a moment before he said: "No, I don't mean that. The arm may get all right in time. It ought to improve, anyway. Give it a lot of massaging, though. Up here . . . dig into these muscles . . . dig right in and work on them every day. It'll hurt . . . but it ought to do you good. Patience and time . . . they work wonders."

"Instead of getting better, it may get worse?" asked Jones.

"Why, no. I hope not. Of course it won't get worse . . . I hope."

"You think it's a bust," insisted Jones. "Go on and let me have it between the eyes."

The doctor was sweating profusely. "Injured nerves are serious things. They have to be cared for, worked over. And . . . even then one cannot always tell."

He put his hand on the big, bare arm of the youth and looked at the stone-white of his face.

"By God, old fellow, I'm sorry!" said the doctor.

Max Brand

"That's all right," said the young man who had said his name was Jones.

"If I were you," continued the doctor, hastily, because he was moved to the heart by the cheerful calm of his patient, "if I were you, I would start at once turning my left hand into a right hand. I'd start in spending hours every day in attempting to make the brain hitch up a straighter wire to the left hand. I'd keep on working with the right, too. I'd never give up hope. But I'd even start trying to write left-handed. It can be learned."

Jones was pulling on his undershirt. He straightened it, dragged over it the thick blue-flannel outer shirt which served also as a coat, except in the most bitter winter weather. Now that he was dressed and had retied the bandanna about his throat, he looked a trifle less formidable. The narrowness of his hips belied the real weight and power of those shoulders, once the shirt obscured their bulging muscles. One might have almost described this man as tall and *slender*.

He picked up his belt, last of all, and buckled it on. It hung loosely, canting high on the left thigh and low over the right, with the time-polished holster of the Colt hanging low down, convenient to the touch of his hand. As his fingers brushed across the worn leather, now, he turned that hand palm up and stood there silently, looking down as though he were seeing it for the first time.

"It's just a wooden leg, you might say," suggested Mr. Jones, in his soft and pleasant voice.

Then he added, as cheerfully as ever: "What do I owe you, Doctor Lindus?"

"Three dollars," said the doctor.

"Ah . . . more than that, I guess. Five dollars would be closer, wouldn't it?" asked Jones. He pulled out a wallet which he had begun to unfasten, but the fingers of his right hand kept fumbling and stumbling and slipping on the strap. He made another very brief pause and looked at that hand again. The smile never failed to curve his lips, slightly, but in the eyes there was a sort of frightened agony. Then, left-handed, he opened the wallet and gave the doctor a bill.

The doctor frowned. "I wanted to add a bit more advice," he said huskily.

"Go right ahead, partner," invited Jones.

"The weather around here . . . it may not be right for that arm of yours," said the doctor. "Summer *or* winter . . . it would hardly do for you. I'd go some place where the altitude is less . . . and the extremes of temperature not so great."

Young Jones was looking fixedly at him, searching his mind, until finally the doctor broke out: "I'd go somewhere else . . . where there aren't so many Martins around!"

One of those pregnant silences continued for a moment. "You know me, Doctor Lindus?" asked the man who had said his name was Jones.

"I know you, Cheyenne," said the doctor.

"You knew me all along?" he asked.

"No. But an idea about you kept building in me, and all at once I knew. If you stay around here, the Martins will certainly get you. They'll never forgive you for the killing of Danny Martin, and the shooting of Chuck."

"They asked for it. What was I to do?"

The doctor brushed away philosophical considerations. "That's all right," he said. "But there are other things. If the Martins got another mob and pulled you down, public opinion would probably call it 'self defense.'"

"Because I'm Cheyenne . . . because some folks call me a gunman? Is that it?"

"You've put a long life into mighty few years," remarked Lindus.

"It's really been a quiet life," answered Cheyenne, "except for some people's foolish talk."

"It seems to me that I can remember a good many times when your life wasn't so quiet. There was that affair of the Tollivers."

"I was just a kid and I got excited when the three of them began to put the pressure on me."

"There was Rip Morgan."

"Rip was a bad *hombre*. And I was young enough to feel that I ought to get myself a little reputation."

"What did I hear about Larue?"

"He was only a Canuck," said Cheyenne.

"And there were two men over in Tombstone. And some others here and there!"

"One of those in Tombstone was a crooked gambler. But I'm not arguing. I just wanted to tell you that it's been a pretty quiet life. I've lived by punching cows, not by shooting men."

"Nevertheless," said the doctor, "if you'll take my advice, you'll disappear out of this part of the country before some of your enemies find out that you've only got a left hand!"

At this, Cheyenne glanced out the window, and the doctor saw the softening of his eyes as they rested on the majestic heights of the nearby mountains.

"You love your range, Cheyenne. Is that it?"

"Well, I've had Old Smoky and some of those other mountains in my eye all my life, Doc."

"You'll have to take 'em out. You'll have to go somewhere and get used to a new landscape for a while . . . till you're cured."

"Cured?" said Cheyenne. And he smiled suddenly at the doctor in a way that brought a lump into the throat of Lindus. "You're right," went on Cheyenne. "I've got to get out. And I'm going to. Thanks, Doc."

He went to the door, put on his hat with his right hand, pulled it down with the left. "So long, Doc," he said.

"Good luck to you, Cheyenne," said the doctor, anxiously.

Chapter Two
Gun Challenge

Outside, in the street, Sideways was still waiting for him with her head high. The gray mare pricked her ears in welcome now, and came toward him as far as the tethering rope would let her. The lines of her beauty and her strength filled his mind as a fine tool fits the hand of an artisan, but above all he loved to see the wild brightness melt out of her eyes when she looked at him after an absence.

Well, before he was safely off this range, he might need all the windy speed of her galloping hoofs, all the strength of her heart. He should, he knew, get out of town at once. Yet he could not start until the shoe that had loosened on her right forefoot was tightened.

He untied the rope and she followed him across the street, making sure that he was indeed her master by sniffing at his hand, at his shoulder, at the nape of his neck. He would have smiled at this persistent affection, but the dread of people for the first time was clotting his blood and benumbing his brain with fear.

Every window seemed an eye that stared at him and perceived instantly that he was not what he had been. His height and his weight were what they had been before, but he was a shell that contained no substance, a machine whose power could not be used. His right hand was gone.

He passed through the open double-doors of the blacksmith shop into the pungent, sulphurous clouds of blue smoke that rolled away from the fire, beside which the blacksmith was swaying the handle of the bellows up and down with the sooty weight of his arm. The smithy, who was big and fat, wiped the sweat off his forehead and left a smudge behind. He was so hot and so fat that grease seemed to distill with his sweat.

"Shoeing all around?" he asked.

"Just tighten up the right fore shoe," said Cheyenne.

He started to make a cigarette, but suddenly changed his mind and crunched the wheat-straw paper inside his left hand, letting the makings dribble to the ground. For no man must be allowed to see the brainless clumsiness of his touch.

He stood at the head of the mare, saying to the smith "Be easy with her. Move your hands slowly or she'll kick your head off."

The blacksmith, with the forefoot of the mare between his knees, was pulling off the loose shoe, wrenching it from side to side. The gray flattened her ears and breathed noisily out of red-rimmed nostrils, until a word from Cheyenne quieted her.

The smoke was rising to the soot-encrusted rafters, and the slanting sun began to illumine the interior of the shop. Which was why the newcomer who stepped just then in from the street looked to be more shadow than human.

But Cheyenne sensed the danger even before he recognized the man, a fellow with wide, heavy jaws and narrow, squinted eyes beneath a sloping forehead. It was Turk Melody. He had been a great friend of Buck Wilson who, only three months before, had made his play to win a great name by matching draws with Cheyenne. He had not wanted to kill that wild young fool. He had put a bullet through Buck's hip. But the bullet had glanced upward, and Buck had died—despite the doctors that Cheyenne had brought to him.

Turk Melody had not been present at the time. He had arrived only in time to look at the dead man and to swear, with his right hand raised, that he would avenge Buck the first time he met Cheyenne. It was a public statement. That was the trouble with it, for men who make public statements on the range often have to die for them.

Turk, as he saw Cheyenne, snatched at his gun. And Cheyenne did nothing. Lightning messages were ripping from his brain to his right hand, and back again. His right hand twitched, but that was all.

Even if he pulled the gun before he was dead, he knew that he would not be able to hit a target with it. Frosty cold invaded him. The back of his neck ached with rigidity. His stomach was hollow. Something like homesickness troubled his heart. It was then he realized that he was afraid!

He could thank God for one thing only—that the smile, however frozen, remained on his face. He was going to die. Turk Melody was going to kill him, driven on to action by the promise he had made to the world.

The blacksmith felt the electric chill of that moment. He straightened suddenly and growled: "Now, what the hell's up?"

At that Turk Melody cried: "Fill your hand, Cheyenne! Damn you . . . fill your hand!"

His voice was a scream. It quivered up and down the scale. And Cheyenne could see that his whole body was shaken.

Fighting his own fear, Cheyenne walked forward slowly: "You poor scared fool," he said. "Your hand's shaking. I don't want to murder you, Melody. You! . . . get out of here before I start something."

The eyes of Turk Melody widened. His face drained of color, became white and drawn. Then his glance slowly wavered to the side and found the blacksmith. It was pitiful, as though he wanted advice, and the blacksmith gave it.

"If this here is Cheyenne," said the smith, "don't you go and make yourself a dead hero. Go on away and wait till you've growed a bit."

The right hand of Turk Melody left his gun. The gun sank slowly, as though reluctantly, into the holster. And then Turk turned his back and walked out of the shop, leading his horse. He had turned his back on praise. He was walking into scorn and infamy.

"No more sense than a mule, that Melody," said the blacksmith.

Cheyenne said nothing. He could not speak. His tongue was frozen to the roof of his mouth, and he dared not turn around at once, for fear that the blacksmith might see the departing shadow of terror on his face.

Chapter Three
Two Kinds of Fear

There was no joy in Cheyenne as he rode out of town, for he knew that a man cannot keep on bluffing forever. Not on his home range, for there were too many fellows like Buck, always ready to gamble with life and death for the sake of making a quick reputation. His eyes were dim as he headed Sideways vaguely towards Old Smoky.

Something began to swell in his heart and, though he kept on smiling, his teeth were set hard. He had heard Blackfeet squaws screaming a dirge for a dead man, a chief, and that lament kept forming in him and rising into his thoughts. For he was dead with life still in him. He had been a master of men. He had always been able to herd them as sheepdogs herd sheep. But now any fifteen-year-old stripling could knock him out of the saddle or beat him hand to hand in fair fight. Moreover, the sheep had felt his teeth too often; they would be ready to rush him and drag him down when they learned that he was helpless. But looking back he could honestly say that he had never sought out trouble. When trouble came his way, he had accepted it. That was all.

He determined to make a compromise between a straight retreat from his home range and a direct return to it. Into it he dared not go, because the Martins would certainly get him. They were a fighting clan, and they would never forgive him for that day when Danny Martin and Chuck attacked him, full of red-eye and murder. He had killed Danny. But Chuck lived, after putting the bullet through Cheyenne's shoulder. With the pain of the wound grinding like teeth at his flesh, he had waited for

Chuck to go on with the gunwork. But Chuck had lain still and played 'possum—the dog! And Cheyenne could not pump lead into a man too yellow to fight.

Well, the Martins would certainly be at his throat if he returned to the range, but he felt that he had to ride once more under the mighty shadow of Old Smoky mountain. He could take a course that angled off the base of the peak and soon find himself headed far into the north. Perhaps in another day he would see the last of his mountain turning blue on the southern horizon. After that, he would pass out into a foreign world.

Clouds began to roll out of the northwest. They closed over the head of Old Smoky. They rolled down across the wide slopes, like the dust of a thousand stampedes roaring into the north.

Cheyenne was in the pass before the shadow swept over him. Looking back, he could see it slide over hill and valley, while the voice of the storm began to reach him, then an occasional rattle of raindrops that made him unstrap his slicker and put it on. Small whirlpools of dust formed over the trail, blew toward him, expanded, and dissolved. The whole sky was darkened, by this time, and the dust which had been sun-whitened was now gray, speckled with black. The acrid smell of it under the rain joined with the wet of the grass. A troop of crows flew low over a hill, flapping their wings in clumsy haste, and dived into a heavy copse.

Then the heart of the storm came over Old Smoky and blotted it out to the feet. Behind that running wall of shadow, glistening with the streaked and sheeted rain, Cheyenne could still draw accurately the picture of the mountains. But it was time to get to shelter. The long southward slant of the rain showed the force of the wind that had hitherto reached him only in occasional gusts. He remembered a nearby cave that as a boy he had often explored and made for it now.

The brush at its entrance had grown taller in the years since he had last seen the cave. His mustang held back, snorting and suspicious, at that mouth of darkness. But a heavy cannon-shot of thunder, followed by a drumroll of distant echoes, drove her forward into Pendleton's Cave. Then the rain fell against the cliff face, like wall against wall, an unending roar of ruin.

Jets of light sprang from heaven to earth. The brush at the cave mouth flashed from blurred shadow into flat silhouette and back again. Hail came, blast on billowing blast of it, making the cave icy cold in a breath or two. So Cheyenne got the little hand-axe out of his saddle pack and chopped down some brush. When he used his right hand, the blade kept turning. Once the force of the stroke knocked the tool out of his nerveless grasp. And his heart sickened as he began the work with his left hand only. There was no sense, no power of direction in that hand. Yet it was surer than the right. It seemed to Cheyenne that half his brain had resided in the exquisite precision, the delicate touch of that hand. Now half of his brain was gone.

Awkwardly, he managed to get a fire going in the cave. He was standing before it, his hands stretched toward the warmth when, outside, a horse whinnied through a thunder roll. Hoofbeats came crackling over the rocks. Cheyenne, now at the mouth of the cave, saw the misty figure of a rider heading toward him. Lightning poured down on the night, cracking the sky with a jagged rent, and the rider swayed to the left, suddenly shrinking.

Cheyenne wondered at that. Riders of the hill trails are not usually ones to fear lightning. But the speed of the horse rushed this stranger into his vision, and he saw at once that it was a girl. She swung out of the saddle and ducked forward as though not rain but bullets were showering around her. Her horse came right in behind her. It went over and touched noses with Cheyenne's mustang, while the girl threw back her dripping slicker and crouched down instantly beside the fire.

She was in a blue funk. She seemed to think that the fire would give her protection from the lightning; the hands she held over the warmth she lifted as extra shields against those sky-ripping thunderbolts!

Cheyenne looked down on her with infinite disapproval. Women had never entered a page of his life except for a sentence or two. If he went to a dance, it was because there was an excitement in the air, and whiskey, and music, and many men with the look of adventure in their eyes. He held his dancing partners lightly, both with the hand and with the heart.

He felt he knew a lot about girls and he had always thought them both weak and foolish. When Cheyenne looked down upon this girl who had sought refuge from the storm, he saw that she had all the weakness of her sex. Her eyes were not bad, because they were the blue of a mountain lake—though they were foolishly large. Her lips had not yet been stiffened and straightened by the labors, the dangers, and pains of life. Her mouth was softly curving, like the mouth of a child. Her first words revealed all her weakness in one breath.

"Isn't it terrible?" she said, and sobbed in fright.

And Cheyenne, with mounting contempt in his heart, suddenly found his thoughts journeying inward through his own soul. The lightning out of the sky filled her with fear. Yet he, like the coward he had become, was ready to run away from the lightning that came from the eyes of angry men. This thought staggered and sickened him. The stature of his soul was no greater than that of the trembling girl beside him and, if he gave her comfort now, it was a cheap gift from a weak nature.

Chapter Four
A Promise to Die!

The sky opened now, like the mouth of a dam, and let fall a blinding cascade of lightning. Thunder shook Old Smoky to the roots. The vibration was great enough to detach a few rocks from the ragged roof of the cave and drop them heavily.

The girl had sprung up as the explosion began. With its continuance she shrank against Cheyenne. He put his arm around her, loosely. She was all full of twitching and shuddering like the hide of a sensitive horse. And, after all, there are even quite a few men, otherwise courageous, who are afraid of thunder and lightning.

"Hey, it's going to be all right," said Cheyenne.

"I . . . I'm afraid!" she whispered, and it took her seconds to get the last word out, she stammered so badly on the "f."

"You want company, eh?" said Cheyenne. "Come here Sideways."

His gray mare came over at once, sniffed at the fire, pricked her ears at the next river of lightning, then gave her attention to the girl. She put one hand up and gripped the mare's mane.

"What's your name?" asked Cheyenne.

She said her name was Dolly.

"Dolly is short for Dorothy, isn't it?" asked Cheyenne. "Well, Dorothy, get hold of yourself."

"I shall . . . I'm going to!" she declared. But she only got a stronger grip on Cheyenne. "I'm going to be all right," she said. "You won't leave me, will you?"

"No," said Cheyenne.

"Oh, what must you think of me? What *can* you think of me?" she moaned. Cheyenne, thinking of his own weakness, colored but said nothing. "Say something," she demanded. "Talk to me! I'll get hold of myself, if I have something besides thunder to listen to."

He sighed. A child might have talked like this. And except for years, of course, she was nothing but a child. He said: "When you came and leaned on me at first, I was sort of reminded of something."

"*Do* tell me," pleaded the girl.

"Yeah, I'm going to," said Cheyenne

A new outbreak of madness in the sky knocked Dorothy into a shuddering pulp again. He patted her shoulder, which seemed to have no bone in it. Strange to say, it was a compound of softness and roundness. Stranger still, from the patting of the girl's shoulder, a ridiculous feeling of comfort and happiness began to run up the arm of Cheyenne to his heart.

"Up Montana way," said Cheyenne, "I was riding one time with some *hombres* who were aiming to run down a big wild mustang herd which didn't have a stallion at the head of it. There was a gray mare, instead. She had black points all around, and she was smart as a hellcat. Many a remuda she busted up and took away the faster half of it."

There was such a frightening downpour of thunder here, that the cave was revealed in one continuing, quivering glare of white brilliance, and the uproar stifled the outcry of the girl. So Cheyenne, with a sigh, sat down on a rock. It would be much easier to endure the leaning in that posture. She sat beside him, using his shoulder and one of her hands to shut out the sight of danger.

"Go on, please . . . don't stop talking," she said.

He went on: "We got on the heels of the herd and followed it for quite a spell, and one day with a good relay of horses, we gave the mustang herd a hard run. Then I discovered that the gray mare was no longer leading. Instead, she'd come back to the rear of the herd and, as the rest of the band shot by, there she was left, standing, looking at us, pricking her ears. It was the queerest thing I ever saw. Horses have fast feet so that they can run away, but it looked as though that she-devil intended to charge us to drive us away from her herd.

"I just had time to notice that she was big with foal when Art Gleason, off on my right, jerked up his rifle and sank a bullet in her. Well, she didn't budge. She didn't even put her ears back. She just stood there and looked.

"Gleason and the rest, they went charging along, but there was something about the way the old girl pricked her ears and faced the world that stopped me. I pulled up and saw the blood running out of her where Gleason's bullet had gone home. I wanted to go up and help her, and try to stop the bleeding, and then I saw that she was hurt where help would do her no good. As a matter of fact, she should have been dying right then and there. You understand?"

"No," said the girl, faintly.

"The maternal instinct . . . it was stronger than death. She was dead, all right. Gleason's bullet had killed her. But she wouldn't die. She kept her ears pricked forward, looking at happy days, it seemed to me. And when the foal was born, that mare laid down and died. While I stood by and wondered over her and damned the buzzards that were beginning to sail into the sky, that foal came over and leaned on me. It was a queer thing . . . soft . . . it was all soft. It poked its nose into my hand and sucked my thumb. It had its legs all spread out to keep on balance. And there I was, a thousand miles from no place."

The lightning shot from the sky in such a mighty stream that all the other displays had been nothing. The thunder plunged like iron horses in an iron valley. But through the tremendous tumult the girl, as though unaware of fear now, threw back her head and cried to Cheyenne: "But what did you do?"

Not by the glow of the fire but by lightning he saw her face suffused and her eyes shining wide open. "I started to go for the nearest ranch," he said. "But the doggone filly started after me, with its legs sprawling every which way. It was the doggondest thing."

"And then?" said the girl.

He found that he had been dreaming the scene all over again, silently. He smiled back into the face of the girl and she smiled, in expectant excitement, in return. "Well, we both got to the ranch," he said, at last. "It was a pretty tight squeeze, and that filly needed a good lot of helping along the way. She pretty near had to be carried the last stretch. But we both got there, and with a few days of care, she began to come around on cow's milk, with some sugar added." He kept on smiling at her, and she smiled back.

"*I* know something!" she said.

"Do you?" said Cheyenne, with something in his voice which had never been there before—an uneasy joy working in his throat.

"Yes, I know something. That filly of the poor gray mare . . . she's the very one you have here! *This* is that same filly grown up!"

"Not so grown up, either," said Cheyenne. "She still doesn't know enough to keep her nose out of my pockets. She'll try anything from Bull Durham to paper money."

"Ah, the darling!" cried the girl, and she sprang up and put her arms around the neck of the gray mare.

Something had been filling the heart of Cheyenne for a long time, perhaps, and now he discovered that it was full to the brim and running over with a foolish excess of happiness. He stood up, also. Thunder pealed more gently, running to a distance in the south. Plainly, the storm was no more than a heavy squall. And now, far beyond the mouth of he cave, he saw a shaft of golden sunlight streaming down on the earth.

They went out with the horses into the open. The northern sky was tumbled white and blue; to the south the storm fled, with its load of thunder.

The girl could hardly leave the gray mare. "What's her name?" asked Dorothy.

"Sideways. Sideways is the way she bucks. She's got

some pretty mean twisters up her sleeve, too."

They mounted and rode out onto the trail. The rain still dripped on the cliffs, and the sun made them shine like dark diamonds.

"You haven't told me your name," she said.

"John Jones," he said.

"Is it? Well, I never would have guessed that. I would have guessed something . . . well, something else."

"Which way?"

"I'm taking the southern pass."

"I ride north," he said gloomily.

"You're not leaving this part of the range? You're not just riding through, are you?" she entreated, and she held out a slim brown hand toward him to prevent the wrong answer.

"Well . . . ," he began.

"I wish you were going to be somewhere around till Saturday," she told him. "There's going to be a dance that day. How I wish you were going to be there!"

"I shall be," said Cheyenne. He listened to his voice say that, and was amazed. It could not be coming from his own throat! If he were to go on living, he must be far away by Saturday.

"You *will* come? How happy I am! The dance is at Martindale."

He heard the word, but would not believe it. The picture of the old town ran again through his mind. He knew every inch of the place, and Martindale knew him. It had been named by the first of the Martin clan to settle in the mountains. It would be far better for him to attend a dance in a nest of rattlesnakes than to go to Martindale.

"And you? Your name?" he asked, slowly.

"I'm Dolly Martin. I'm Ned Martin's daughter," she said.

He pulled off his hat and took her hand in his. The warmth of her touch seemed to re-sensitize that half-dead right hand of his. "Saturday night," he said.

"I'll be looking for you every minute. Thank you a lot. I'm sorry I was so silly."

He could not believe what he was saying: "Lots of men are afraid of lightning, too. A fellow can't help being that way."

"It was a beautiful story!" said Dorothy Martin. "I loved it. I love Sideways, too, the darling. Good bye!"

That was Monday. It gave Cheyenne five days to get his right hand in working shape.

Chapter Five
Preparation

He found a deserted shack up on the south shoulder of Old Smoky and lived there. The forage for Sideways was good. There was a bright little cascade, making its own thunder and lightning, not far away. As for game, he could go to chosen spots and wait, his revolver, in his left hand, steadied across a rock until meat walked into view. This was not sportsmanship, but perhaps he was never again to be a sportsman.

He began his days with the first faint light of the morning and ended them very late, by fire light. He practiced writing, left-handed and right-handed—and found that left-handed was easier. He tried his axe left-handed and right-handed. Left-handed was easier. Whatever he did with his right hand seemed to blur his brain with the effort. It was like walking over a straight road that is deep with mud.

Once—it was on the third day—as he patiently worked the pencil with his left hand over the paper, he looked down at the formless, scrawling line that he had made and suddenly leaped up with an oath. He beat his fists against the wall of the shack and cursed the Martins, the girl, the doctor—and finally himself.

Afterwards he went out into the sun and sat down. The sun was hot. The wind carried life into his nostrils. Off at the side, he saw from the corner of his eye the silver flash of the cascade which kept on talking, high or low, by day and by night. It was better, he decided, to live up here, secluded, than to go down among men and be slaughtered. He could see now that, although there was a special peril in Martindale, there were other perils in all places for him. His hand had been too heavy, and it had fallen on too many people.

He could remember, now, the men he had fought against in other days—men with white, strained faces, distraught and desperate as they faced odds against which they knew they could not triumph. He had thought, in those other times, that these fellows were simply cowards. Now he knew better. He could feel the strain coming into his own face, as he merely thought of undertaking battle against normal fighting men.

On Wednesday he made up his mind that he would not go down to Martindale, no matter what he had promised the girl. On Thursday he was assured that it would be madness for him to enter that town. On Friday he stood out with his revolver in his right hand and tried three shots at a big rock. Twice the bullets hit the air. One slug hit the ground ten feet away from the base of the boulder.

Sick-faced, he stared down at hand and gun. He tried left-handed. All three shots hit the rock, but he had to fire slowly. In the time he needed for firing one shot with any accuracy, he could have poured in eight or ten in the old days, flicking home the shots with an instinct that was like touch.

Saturday morning a deer actually walked across the clearing. He had a chance for three shots—left-handed. The third wounded the deer in the shoulder. It fled, three-legged, for a mile. He had to follow and put it out of its pain. Then he had to cut up the carcass—left-handed—and bear the burden of the meat back to the little shack. Four shots to kill a deer!

But the best part of this was that he had plenty to do in fire-and-sun drying the venison. He would keep himself occupied while this day wore away, and the time of the dance with it. Then the sun went down.

He tried to busy himself about the shack, but the beauty of the sunset drew him to the door where he stood at watch. That turbulent rising of mountains west and north, that far flowing of the hills to the south made his

Yellow Dog

mind flow that way to the picture of unseen Martindale.

He had been in that very dance hall, more than once.
He knew every house and shop in the town. He had been
a welcome visitor there. But now Danny Martin was
dead, and Chuck Martin walked with a limp. Every time
Chuck Martin limped, the Martins were sure to set their
teeth and renew their bitter, silent resolve to take his life.

He began to think of Danny Martin, handsome and savage and treacherous, making an easy living through his
crooked skill with the cards. Try as he might, he could
not be sorry that he had planted a few ounces of lead in
Danny's lithe young body.

They would be lighting their lamps in Martindale, now.
They'd be polishing the floor of the barn which served as
a dance hall. And the girls of the town would be deco-
rating the old place, stringing long sweeping lines of
twisted, bright-colored paper streamers along the rafters
and walls.

Cheyenne took a step outside the door of the shack.
The night was coming. It was rising out of the earth, and
the day was departing from the burning sky. There was
a coldness and sickness in him. And he knew that that
was the stranger: fear. But there was a joy in him, too;
and that, he knew, was the picture of Dolly Martin. He
found himself saddling Sideways.

Then he was scrubbing his hands, working on the nails
to get the impacted grease out from under them. He was
taking a bath in cold water, using roughness of hard rubbing in the place of hot water and soap. Yet all the time
he told himself that he would never be such a fool as to
go down to the dance in Martindale. And all the time he
knew that he would go.

Chapter Six
Cheyenne Rides to Town

Cheyenne, riding steadily through the night, tried at first to keep his mind from Martindale and the dire test he knew awaited him there. He thought of the old days when he had been as strong as other men; of the night in Tombstone when he had won five hundred dollars—and killed a man. But he found scant comfort in such memories and the new, cold fear in his heart at last drove all other thought from him. After all, was he not like a condemned prisoner passing to the gallows?

He expected to find himself tense, trembling when he entered the street of the town, but as a matter of fact the moment he passed the first house he was at ease. Not without pain, but it was as though he had squared off at another man and received the first blow which shocks the panic out of the mind.

Then he heard the music which throbbed out of the barn. He heard the burring sound of the bass viol and the thin shrill song of the violin, and above all the long and brazen snarling of the slide trombone. The beat of the drums was almost lost. It was a pulse in the air, and that was all.

Under the trees in front of the Slade barn the long hitching racks had been built. And horses were everywhere. He heard them snorting and stamping—those were the colts. And he saw, also the old veterans of the saddle, down-headed, pointing one rear hoof.

He picked a gap in a rack near the lighted entrance, dismounted. Other men were about him, getting ready to enter the barn. He saw a gleam as of metal, and his heart leaped. But it was only the sheen of a bottle tilting slowly at the lips of a man.

He walked in toward the door, passing many figures in the darkness. He came into the little framed off ante-room where coats and slickers and guns were left. He hung up his hat and his gun belt. The room was an armory.

The orchestra had paused. Now it began again. And the idlers were drawn suddenly back into the barn to the dance. He went up to the window and saw Jud Wilkins selling tickets. Jud was a long-jawed humorist with twinkling eyes. But his eyes did not twinkle when he saw Cheyenne.

"My Lord . . . ," he murmured, then he pushed a ticket across the sill and took the money.

"Sort of a warm night for the dance, eh?" said Cheyenne.

"Yeah . . . kind of . . . but . . . my Lord!" muttered Jud Wilkins.

Cheyenne went inside. The roof of the barn was so high and black that the illumination under the lower rafters looked like rising rust. It was a tag dance, and he saw men running into the crowd and touching other men, sometimes slapping them resounding thwacks on the back or the shoulders. No one seemed to notice him. Then he found Dorothy Martin.

She was dancing with big Lew Parkin, who danced slowly. There was a slight bend to his head and shoulders, as though in proper reverence to his partner. She seemed to be enjoying her dance with Lew Parkin. She kept looking up at him and smiling a little. But now and again her glance went to the door of the barn.

Now her look fell straight on Cheyenne, and the smile she sent him set his heart to a thumping. He walked through the crowd, stepping lightly.

Some voice, a man's voice, said behind him: "Excuse me . . . a gent just went by that looked almost like. . . ."

Well, that would be the beginning of the whisper and the deadly preparation for the fight. But it seemed to

Cheyenne that this would be the easiest night of a long lifetime for death. He felt that when bullets struck him he could still be laughing. In fact, the faint smile which was characteristic of him was on his lips and in his eyes as he came to the girl and tapped Lew Parkin on the shoulder.

Lew stepped back and almost threw up his hands. "You?" he gasped.

He looked like a hero in a cheap play, confronting the villain.

The girl stepped into Cheyenne's arms, and they moved off. His feet found the swinging rhythm of the waltz. He usually danced on the outer edge of the floor, but he kept to the inside, now, on the verge of that slight vacuum which always forms toward the center of a big dance floor.

"I was hoping that you'd come earlier," she said. "But this is better than nothing at all. Did you have a long distance to come? I've saved supper for you. You'll have supper with me, John? Won't you? I haven't told anyone about you. Not a soul. Not even mother. I want you to be a surprise, I didn't even talk about being driven into a cave. No one knows a thing. How surprised they will all be! People are looking at you, John. They're looking almost as though they know you. But you haven't said . . . you're going in to supper with me?"

"I can't stay," said Cheyenne. "I can only stay for this one dance."

"Only for this one? Only *one* dance, John!"

The light threw the sheen of her hair down over her forehead, over her eyes. And if one had been unable to understand a word that she spoke, it would have been a delight, nevertheless, to watch the parting and the closing of her lips.

The fluff of her sleeve fell back up her arm almost to the shoulder. Other women had sharp elbows, and the flesh of a girl's arm pinches away toward the shoulder, or else it hangs flabby. But hers was rounded, brown. She seemed to be brown all over.

"How did you get so brown?" he asked her.

"We have a swimming pool behind the house."

She laughed a little and looked up at him. "We're clear around the floor, and no one has tagged you yet."

"No one is going to tag me," said Cheyenne.

"But look, John . . . half the people are off the dance floor!"

More than half had stopped dancing. In a tag dance, every girl ought to be busy; but now they were drifting off the floor, looking back over their shoulders. The music of the slide trombone screeched and died in the middle of a note.

"What's wrong?" asked the girl. "What's happening, John?"

Chapter Seven
One Against the Martins

Everyone in the big room seemed to be asking the same question at the same moment; and the rest of the crowd rapidly stopped dancing and drifted away to the sides of the barn. The orchestra died away piece by piece, following the example of the slide trombone. The drums, the cornet, the bass viol went silent one by one, and the only music which remained was the thrilling voice of the violin.

The violinist was old Tom McKenzie, seventy years old with a rag of white beard on his chin and eyes which still danced faster than young feet ever performed to his music. The good old man had been sitting down, sawing away at the strings with his head canted a little to one side. But when he saw the crowd breaking up and pouring away from the single pair that remained, he jumped to his feet and began to play such a waltz as he never had played before to woo those two dancers to continue.

The drummer snarled at his shoulder: "Don't you be a fool, Pop. There's gonna be guns bangin' away, pretty soon. Out yonder, that's Cheyenne who's dancing with Dolly Martin."

"Is that Cheyenne? Well, God bless him! If he's gonna die, he'll die to all the music that I can give him!" answered Pop McKenzie, and he made his fiddle whistle more sweetly and loudly than before.

"What is it?" the girl was repeating to Cheyenne. "Everyone has stopped . . . even the music . . . except Pop McKenzie. Do you know what's wrong?"

"I know what's wrong," he said.

"Please tell me."

"I'm what's wrong."

"You? John Jones?"

"I'm not John Jones."

He held her a bit closer. "What do you care about the name? Well, you'll start hating me in another five minutes, Dorothy. But up to then, while the fiddle plays, why shouldn't we dance?"

"I'll never start hating you," she answered him.

Her father was a Martin, he knew, who had moved into the community only a year or two before, and perhaps the reputation of Cheyenne might not be such an outrage to his mind and to his daughter as to the rest. But they knew—all men knew—about the recent killing of Danny Martin.

"I'm a man that all the Martins are bound to curse," he told her.

"All the Martins? Then I'm not really a Martin. How they are staring!"

"Dolly!" shouted a loud voice.

Cheyenne saw a tall, gaunt, stern-featured man standing at the side of the hall, holding up a hand. He was of middle age. There was a brightness in his eyes that made Cheyenne recognize him as the father of Dorothy Martin.

"Dolly, stop dancing! You hear me?"

She stiffened inside the arms of Cheyenne.

"I've got to stop," she said.

"One more round. It'll be the last one," said Cheyenne.

She came back to him, though she said: "It's my father!"

"I know it," said Cheyenne.

"Ah, but they're staring at us."

"It's a good way to use their eyes."

He hardly needed to touch her with his hands, she was so close, so balanced in a perfect rhythm. And all about them he heard a rising sound such as the muttering of trees far off across a forest. But this was composed of the voices of men and women. It gathered in strength. Tall Ned Martin was striding across the floor.

"Dolly, d'you mind what you're doing . . . dancing with Cheyenne?" he shouted.

One might have thought that she had known the name all the while. There was no touch or stir of shock in her. He looked into her eyes, and they were the unalterable blue of mountain lakes.

"Did you hear him?" he asked.

"I heard," said the girl.

"And there's no difference?"

"There'll never be any difference," she said.

Long ago, years and years before, he had thought she was no more than a child. He began to understand, now, that he'd been wrong.

They moved straight past the outstretched arm and the stunned face of Ned Martin. Some of the men were starting out from their places along the wall as Cheyenne stopped in front of the entrance. The anteroom was crowded. Men out there had guns in their hands. They had grimly waiting faces. Between the barn and Sideways there was a distance of thirty steps which could be thirty deaths for him.

"Look," said Cheyenne, "you're the bigger half of things from now on. It may not be long, but you're the bigger half of things. Good bye!"

"You came because I asked you," she was saying. "You knew. . . ."

He turned on his heel. If she had understood why he had come, it would make the going easier.

They were all there about him. He saw Chuck Martin back in the crowd with his head lowered a little. And as he saw the face of Chuck, the right arm of Cheyenne seemed as heavy and lifeless as lead. He remembered how Chuck had fired the bullet on that other day, dropping to his knees behind a table, where the return fire of Cheyenne had made him sprawl on the floor.

He saw the Glosters, father and son. They were Martins, to all intents and purposes. Everyone in Martindale lived in the town because they were bound together by strong ties of blood. Fifty men were ready for Cheyenne.

He walked right into their ranks, thronging the door into the anteroom. They receded on either side of him. He said: "All right, boys. Look me over. And bid up my price. There's only one head of me, but I want the price of a herd."

They spilled away on either side, like water from the prow of a ship. And then he was standing buckling on his gun belt.

Someone said: "You grab him, Charlie. Dive at his knees!"

Charlie Martin kept scowling, his huge shoulders stirring, but he could not quite force himself to take the final step.

Out of the dance room Dorothy Martin cried: "Let me go to him, Father. He came here because I asked him. I didn't know . . . and he wouldn't explain. If anything happens to him. . . ."

"Something is gonna happen to him!" cried Charlie Martin.

Cheyenne pulled his hat over his eyes and walked up to the speaker. With his left hand, he struck Charlie across the face. The blow left a white patch between the cheekbone and the chin. "Why don't you move a hand?" asked Cheyenne, then added: "Give me room . . . stand back, will you?"

They stood back. The sound of the blow which Charlie had endured without protest still seemed to be echoing through their brains. They had chosen big Charlie for a leader, and Charlie Martin was remembering too well that the gun of Cheyenne was a fatal thing. Perhaps he had courage enough to fight and to die but he could not be a leader. He fell back, and the others receded around him.

That was how Cheyenne came to the outer edge of the crowd. Between that edge of that sea of danger and Sideways there was one open space. He would die as he crossed it, Cheyenne knew. The bullets would strike him from behind.

"Dolly!" called the frantic voice of Ned Martin. "Where you going? Come back here . . . !"

Then she was outside, running toward Cheyenne. She was a flash of white coming to him. She put an arm around him. She walked, leaning against him, looking back at the mass of her armed kinsmen.

"They won't dare to shoot, now . . . but faster, faster, Cheyenne!"

"You ain't gonna let him get loose?" yelled Chuck Martin. "Oh, you damned rats, you ain't gonna let him get loose, are you? Gimme a chance to get through! Lemme get at him!"

There was a stirring and a movement in the crowd. Men began to exclaim. Everyone had a voice and a thought. None was the same. And always Ned Martin, pushing forward among the rest, was shouting to his daughter to return.

But she stood with Cheyenne at the side of his mare. "Only because I asked you, would you have come into this!" she said. "Ah, John, you could have died! Be quick! Take Sideways. Oh, Sideways, carry him safe and fast!"

There was need for speed. The Martins, having been held by the hypnotic power of this man's reputation, had remained with all their strength dammed up in front of the dance hall. Now that he was at a distance, perhaps he was smaller in their eyes. They came out with a rush, and their voices rose in one increasing, gathering volume. But Cheyenne, aslant in the saddle, was already making Sideways fly down the street through the night.

A good bluff could be made to stick. Cheyenne carried that lesson away with him, as Sideways cut swiftly along the dark trail. Perhaps, with consummate skill and nerve, he might be able to go the rest of his life without being brought closer to a showdown than he had been at that moment in Martindale.

He lived! There was not a scratch on him to show what he had done. And the thought of Dorothy Martin rollicked through his mind like the music of game old Pop McKenzie. Once more he realized that he should take the northern trail. But he was more than ever loathe to leave. If he could continue to bluff his way out of situations as tight as that one tonight. . . . So he went straight back to the shack on the side of Old Smoky.

Chapter Eight
Friendly Warning

He awakened the next morning with the sense of something missing. Before he tasted food, he sat down at his table and wrote a letter. He could not sweep it off in a few easy gestures, as letters had formerly been for him. The right hand could not manage the pen. Therefore, with the left, he printed out the words as neatly as he could.

Dear Dorothy:
    You pulled me through the worst of it. You were great.
    I'm not riding north. This range is good enough for me as long as you want me on it. If you can see me, say when or where. Address me at General Delivery, Crooked Foot.

                    Yours,
                    Cheyenne

Instead of cooking a breakfast, he took some jerky and chewed it on his way down the mountain to Crooked Foot, on the western side of the peak. There he mailed the letter to Miss Dorothy Martin, at Martindale. The whole sound of the name was different to him, now. A light had been shed from within upon all the Martins, young and old. They were distinguished people in the eyes of Cheyenne.

In the days that followed, Cheyenne fell into a frenzy of labor again. It had been important enough before to restore his right hand and put cunning in his left; but now there was a double necessity, for he carried the voice of Dolly Martin in his ear, and the picture of Dolly Martin in the forefront of his brain. He would not willingly have been without that extra weight, but because of it he wanted to redouble his strength.

Once an hour he massaged his right arm, chiefly about the scar tissue in the shoulder. He used hot water, as much as he could stand, then kneaded the flesh with grease. Sometimes sharp tingles shot through the entire arm as his fingers touched a nerve. After each massage the arm was sure to feel lighter, more alive.

And every day there was the constant practice. He used his gun with either hand. He tried chopping wood, hewing to a line also, with either hand. And he was constantly writing, big and small. The result was that the left began to improve rapidly. When he used axe or gun in it, he no longer had such a strange feeling of being off balance, of being only half present. But in the right hand he could see little improvement or none at all.

He endured that disappointment without the leaden falling of his heart which he had felt at first. This was a task that might take a year, two years. It was one to be persisted in. And he had a goal before him.

After three days he went down to the post office in Crooked Foot, but there was no letter waiting for him at General Delivery. He came slowly back up the hill, walking most of the way. He liked to have the pretty head of Sideways at his shoulder, nodding as she worked up the slope. Whenever he looked at the gray mare now, he would think of Dolly Martin, and that made him turn perhaps fifty times a day and whistle to her, so that she would jerk up her head from grazing and look back at him with those bright, steady, fearless eyes.

Old Sam was waiting at the shack when he got there. Sam was the trapper of Old Smoky. He was associated with the mountain almost as closely as the mists that blew around its head. When Cheyenne came in, the old fellow was leaning his height above the stove, cooking. He had bacon in the pan along with plenty of squirrel

121

meat. Squirrels are good eating if you know how to cook them properly.

Sam, without turning his head, greeted Cheyenne by name.

"Eyes in the back of your head, Sam?" asked Cheyenne.

Sam turned slowly. His face was covered with beard that began just below the eyes. It was like gray wool, never barber-trimmed, but hacked off to a convenient length from time to time with a sharp knife. The result was a series of gray knobs and hollows.

"Cheyenne," he said, "there's a deer out yonder, somewhere. I got a look at it through the door a while back. Go and fetch it in."

Cheyenne went outside. It was the heat of the day, and a gray mist was rising from the ground that had recently been soaked with rain. Only the mountains close by could be seen; the more distant hills were lost. He hunted casually up the mountain for the deer, then turned a bit to the east and circled back toward the hut to report failure.

He was drawing near the shack when saw a man skulking ahead of him from rock to rock and from bush to bush, with a rifle pushed before him. Cheyenne, frowning, shifted the revolver to his left hand.

"After something, partner?" he asked.

The other jumped. As he turned, Cheyenne had sight of a handsome young face as brown as his own. But the sudden start of the stranger made him step wrong. A stone rolled from under his feet. His rifle exploded in mid-air and its owner rolled twenty feet down the slope before he was able to halt his fall.

Then he stood up, dizzily. "Kind of didn't expect you behind me," he said.

"Were you expecting me in front?" demanded Cheyenne.

"I was deer-stalking," said the other. He came up the slope in small steps, the way a mountaineer should do.

"Good thing you weren't carrying dynamite," said Cheyenne. "Time for you to eat?"

"I could eat raw meat," said the stranger.

"You can have cooked squirrel instead," said Cheyenne. "Come along."

He took the stranger into his shack. "I'm John Jones," he said. "This is Old Sam, who owns Old Smoky."

"Jim Willis is my name," said the stranger, and instantly made himself useful in bringing wood to feed a failing fire in the stove.

"You seen a deer out there, did you?" asked Old Sam.

"Coming over the eastern shoulder. I thought it must be heading this way. Of course, if I'd known about the cabin being here, I would have cut down the slope and across the ravines. That's where he is, by now. A big devil," he commented, ruefully.

"You from these parts?" asked Old Sam, as he began to dish out food.

"I'm from all around," said Willis.

They sat down to eat in front of the cabin. Cheyenne found himself operating on the meat without thought. The last thing that he wanted was to permit people to see his more than childish clumsiness with a fork; but without thought he had already skewered a squirrel with an iron fork held daggerwise, while he slowly carved the meat with the knife in his left. Once having started, it was foolish to try to hide the facts; Willis had already marked them with a blue-eyed stare that sent ice-worms up the spine of Cheyenne. But Old Sam was too busy talking about the reduction in the bounty on wolves to take heed of other things, apparently.

Willis went on to find his venison immediately after lunch. He thanked the two hosts, and was gone quickly.

But Old Sam remained to smoke a pipe. "Some folks would have stayed to clean up the dirt they made," he suggested.

"There's only a tin plate and a cup and a fork," said Cheyenne.

"Little things make a big difference, sometimes," observed the trapper. "Right hands, is one of them. Who took your arm off at the shoulder, Cheyenne?"

The blunt question made Cheyenne start. "It's a little

out of kilter, is all. I . . . sprained the shoulder a while back."

"Sprained it?" said the other. "Humph!"

Then he went on, as he finished his pipe and rose to go: "You'd think that a gent that comes from all around would be finding his venison down on the hills, without having to stalk all the way up the side of Old Smoky."

"Something wrong about that Willis?" asked Cheyenne, sharply.

"I dunno," said Sam. "I was just thinking."

"Thinking what?"

"That they've lowered the bounty on wolves, but there's still a mighty high bounty on a lot of human scalps."

"What'd you mean by that, Sam?"

"Well, there's some gents that are free targets. Some have a bounty on their heads that'll be paid by the law, and some have a bounty that's only the glory that the killer gets."

Cheyenne stared. "Meaning me?" he asked.

"Son," said Old Sam, "I been looking down through the brush up there day after day and seen you waltzing around down here. I seen you shooting. I seen you chopping wood. And that right arm of yours ain't worth a damn. Me seeing it don't matter, but another gent has seen it, now. If I was you, I'd head right *pronto* for some healthier climate."

Chapter Nine
Bitter Medicine

Cheyenne determined to take Old Sam's good advice and move on, while he still could. Also, he definitely shifted the holster which carried his Colt from the right thigh to the left. Since one stranger knew that his right hand was a numb, half-dead thing, would not the whole range know it soon? It was time for him to travel. He would, he decided, go south, passing the town of Crooked Foot so that he might inquire once more for a letter at General Delivery.

Crooked Foot was well away from the realm of the Martins, but even in this town there was danger. It was not from the Martins only that he could expect trouble. That was why he spent one solid hour on the shoulder of the mountain working with the gun in his left hand. What he should have learned before became apparent now. Any attempt at speed was fatal. The swift throw of the gun ruined the aim but, if he pulled out the Colt with a calm and unhurried precision, he could rock the hammer with a touch of his thumb and crash a bullet into a target almost as accurately as he had been able, in the old days, to turn loose the deadly stream of lead from the right.

It was consolation, but a small one. For in that interval which was filled with deadly slowness, any man familiar with the quick draw was certain to begin pumping lead into him. And how did men quarrel? A chair pushed screaming back from a card table, followed swiftly by the thunder of guns.

Speed was the thing that meant life or death, and for speed he needed brains in his fingers. But the brains of his right hand were gone; and the left, it seemed, would never be more than a half-wit!

It was hard to keep smiling on the way down to Crooked Foot that day, but he managed it. Half the strength of character is the force of habit, perhaps. It was a day half dark, because of the steaming clouds that poured away from the white head of Old Smoky. Crooked Foot itself lay in the shadow and Cheyenne, with a rather childish touch of superstition, felt that this was a friendly omen.

But at the post office there was nothing. He had turned gloomily away from the door of the little building when a bright voice hailed him—a cheerful voice with just a slight element of strain in it, which might be surprise only. It was Willis, striding across the street toward him, waving a hand.

"Hello, Jones," he said. "Glad to see you again! Step in and have a shot of red-eye with me, will you?"

Cheyenne accepted with a wave of his hand. He was still lost in wonder because his letter to the girl had brought no response. It was the sort of a note that demanded an answer. It was the sort of a note she would have been sure to answer, he kept telling himself.

They went into Tom Riley's saloon. Half a dozen cowpunchers were in there, off the range. It was a bad season with less work to be had than there were workers. In the old days Cheyenne would not have worried about that. No matter how pinched a rancher's wallet might be, he was always glad to find room for a man like Cheyenne. But all of that was ended now.

He might be a damned dishwasher, somewhere. No, because he'd break too many dishes. In some far away camp, he'd become the clumsy greenhorn—the "Lefty" of the outfit.

He was at the bar, leaning not his left but his right elbow on the varnished top of it. He took the whiskey.

"Here's how," they said together in deep, rather apologetic voices, putting down that brown-stained fire at the same moment.

As he put the glass back on the bar, Cheyenne saw that the eyes of Willis were dropping to his left thigh, where the Colt now rode. There was a meaning in that glance. There was a stinging meaning in it.

"Have one on me," suggested Cheyenne.

Willis did not answer. A cold light made his blue eyes paler. His nostrils flared.

Then an unseen man entered through the swinging door.

"Slip Martin!" he called. "What you doin' in this part of the range? Why . . . ?"

"Hello, yourself," said the man who had called himself Willis. But his eyes never left the face of Cheyenne. And he raised his voice to say in the snarling tone which means one thing only: "You're Cheyenne!"

It was the invitation to the fight. Old Sam had been right. There was no good in this "Willis." He had not been stalking deer on the shoulder of the mountain. No, it had been other game that he had been after. A scalp with a price of high glory on it.

But how had he known that his quarry was on Old Smoky? How *could* he have known that Cheyenne was near Crooked Foot, unless the girl had published her information?

"Cheyenne!" someone said in a corner of the saloon. "It is Cheyenne."

"If it's Cheyenne," said Tom Riley, behind the bar, "and if you're really a Martin, don't you go and make a damn' fool of yourself. Don't you go and get your insides spilled all over my floor."

"Keep away!" shouted Slip Martin.

He leaned forward a little. His right hand hovered, wavered like a stooping bird, over his gun. It was not a clumsy, half-witted left. It was a right hand that was poised there.

"Keep back and gimme room!" Slip Martin was crying. "I got him where I want him. I'm gonna open him up, and I'm gonna show you that Cheyenne's a dirty, sneaking, yellow dog!"

Cheyenne said nothing. Slip Martin had him. There was no doubt about that. He was gone. He was already as good as dead. And somehow that would have been all right, too—if only the girl had written back to him, if only that hollow uncertainty and disappointment had not been in his soul.

With every second of his silence, of his movelessness, he could see a savage hysteria of joy working more and more deeply into the face of Slip. The man looked like a beast now.

"If you're a man, and not a dirty, low, sneakin' murderer, go for your gun! Fill your hand, or I'll. . . ."

Slip paused there, trembling on the verge of the draw. And Cheyenne did not move.

"My God," said a sick voice, "Cheyenne's gonna take water!"

It was only a murmur, but it fitted perfectly into the sickness of Cheyenne's soul.

"Yeah . . . ," gasped Slip Martin. "I was right." Murder was in his eyes, and then something more cruel appeared there. "I was right. You're only a yellow dog!"

He took a quick half step forward and flicked the back of his left hand across the face of Cheyenne. It was the ultimate insult. Cheyenne thought of Charlie Martin in the crowd at the dance. Charlie had stood white and appalled, working physically to burst away from the controlling hand of awe that gripped him. But he, Cheyenne, was still smiling. The smile would be the most horrible of all. Punch-drunk men in the ring smile like that as they stagger before the conqueror.

"He is!" said someone. "He's yellow. Cheyenne's taking water!"

Cheyenne straightened. He turned to the swing-door. He turned toward all those faces—his back was to the gun of Slip Martin who had called himself "Willis."

The world would never know how Slip had learned that this famous gunfighter was now helpless. Slip Martin would become famous. It was better than shooting a

FREE BOOKS CERTIFICATE!

YES! I want to subscribe to the Leisure Western Book Club. Please send my 4 FREE BOOKS. Then, each month, I'll receive the four newest Leisure Western Selections to preview FREE for 10 days. If I decide to keep them, I will pay the Special Members Only discounted price of just $3.36 each, a total of $13.44. This saves me between $3 and $6 off the bookstore price. There are no shipping, handling or other charges. There is no minimum number of books I must buy and I may cancel the program at any time. In any case, the 4 FREE BOOKS are mine to keep—at a value of between $17 and $20! Offer valid only in the USA.

Name_____

Address_____

City_____ State_____

Zip_____ Phone_____

Biggest Savings Offer!

For those of you who would like to pay us in advance by check or credit card—we've got an even bigger savings in mind. Interested? Check here. ☐

If under 18, parent or guardian must sign.
Terms, prices and conditions subject to change. Subscription subject to acceptance. Leisure Books reserves the right to reject any order or cancel any subscription.

▼ Tear here and mail your FREE book card today! ▼

PLEASE RUSH
MY FOUR FREE
BOOKS TO ME
RIGHT AWAY!

Leisure Western Book Club
P.O. Box 6613
Edison, NJ 08818-6613

man—to make him back down by the sheer force of cold, hard nerve.

Between Cheyenne and the door there stretched the distance of five paces, but they were five eternities to him. On either side were the horrified faces, but the grin of a ghastly pleasure was beginning to dawn on some of them.

This was a thing to remember. This was a thing to be talked about. Eye-witnesses of the fall of Cheyenne would be valued all over the range. And hungry-eyed men would listen, their lips curling with disdain. And other men of guns and might throughout the mountains would listen with horror, wondering if their own nerve might one day run out of them like water through a sieve.

He got to the swing-door, pushed slowly through it into the open day. He would never again be a happy man. He would fear the eye of every man, because every man might know. He halted, standing stiff and straight.

It was better to go back into the saloon and have the thing over with. It was better to rush back. Then he heard the outbreak of the voices inside, a noise that rose, and one man began to laugh, pealing laughter.

"Slip!" shouted one. "That was the finest, coldest piece of nerve that I ever seen. You're the greatest fellow that ever rode this range."

The king was dead. Another king was reigning. . . .

Cheyenne knew that now, if ever, he ought to ride south. He knew—but the face of Old Smoky, above him, was like that of an old friend. He turned toward it for comfort, and kept traveling up the trail that direction.

A cottontail jumped up from behind a rock. He pulled the revolver with his left hand and counted: "One!" Then he fired. The cottontail turned over in mid-leap, struck a rock heavily, and lay still, a blur of red and fluffy gray. Cheyenne pulled Sideways over to the spot and picked up the meat.

If he practiced with a rifle, he might become a hunter, because his eye seemed even better than ever. It had to be, now that the hand was gone. But whatever he hunted, it could never be a man.

Chapter Ten
"Coward's Brand"

Every day Cheyenne tried to leave Old Smoky. Every day the thought of the outer world was poison in his brain. But on the evening of the third day, he went down the trail at last to make a third and final try at the post office in Crooked Foot. He came in from behind the building, waited until there was no one in sight, then walked in to ask. The postmaster was a cripple, with a pale and sneering face. His deformity was in his eyes as well as in his body.

"You're John Jones, are you?" he asked. He leaned forward a little to scan the man. "You *look* big enough!" he sneered. Then he threw a letter across the counter. It skidded down and hit the floor.

Cheyenne said nothing. He picked up the letter and ripped it open. The address was in carefully formed, delicate writing. The brief note was written with the same school-care, like a specimen for a copy-book.

Dear Mr. Jones, or Cheyenne:
I thought you were a man. The Martins have no use for cowards.

Yours very truly,
D. M.

Cheyenne came out into the early darkness with the paper in his hand. On the edge of the village he read the thing again by match light. The matches kept shaking, and the paper kept shaking. He lighted a dozen matches, reading and re-reading the brief note.

Yellow Dog

"I thought you were a man. The Martins have no use for cowards."

That, he thought, was because she was a Thoroughbred. Common people have common reactions. They are open to pity and foolishness. So was she, until the crisis came. But in the pinch she would show the steel.

She was the sort to fill a man with a gentle happiness. But in time of need would she not be as stern and strong as any man? She would be like a child among her children, one day, until the emergencies came. And then they would see her ready for battle. He could see the picture of her altering, her head raising, her eyes changing.

"The Martins have no use for cowards!"

He had no use for a coward either. He pulled out the Colt and put the cold hard muzzle of it between his teeth. It was not fear that kept him from shooting, because everything was finished. His world was reduced to the horse that he rode on. But there was suddenly a good practical reason against this destruction of himself. Yonder there was that consummate traitor—Slip Martin—big and brown and blue-eyed and handsome. He was famous in his world, now. Would it not be better to die trying to repay Slip for the thing that had happened, for the perfection of Slip's treachery? The more he thought of this, the more convinced he became that it was the thing to do.

Slip would kill him, of course. But if he could brace himself against he shock of the bullets—if he could stand straight against a wall so that the impact of the lead would not knock him this way and that—then he might, as he died, drive one bullet fired by the left hand through the heart of Slip. It was better to die trying. He turned the head of he mare toward Martindale, far away.

As he rode, he tried to keep his mind off the letter from Dolly. It was well enough to call it the fine scorn of the Thoroughbred, but there was another name for it, also. "Coward" is strong language. After the cave and the dance at Martindale, "coward" was too strong. He put the letter inside his shirt. The crinkling of it there against his skin would help him, in the last moment, to stand straight against the wall, and shoot back.

So he drifted Sideways slowly through the night. It seemed to him that there would remain only one regret when he stood against the wall and fought his last fight. That regret would be for Sideways. Some other man would have her.

When Cheyenne came into the town, he let the mare swing into a canter, because it was not his purpose to be spotted in some ray of lamplight and so have the alarm spread before he was ready for it. The scene of his death he had selected with care on the way from Old Smoky. It was to be in Jim Rafferty's saloon. He had had his beer in Rafferty's many a time, back in the days when he was only a youngster, a growing name. Rafferty had been a friend, then. He was big, burly. He had been an ex-prizefighter, and at the end of his barroom there was a narrow blank wall. Against that wall, Cheyenne would stand and take whatever was coming to him.

When he pulled up in front of Rafferty's, no other horses were standing at the racks. He got down, threw the reins—why make sure that Sideways waited for him in that spot, or in any spot?—and he lingered for an instant beside the good mare. There were enough splintered rays of lamplight to show him the outline of her head and the gleam of her eyes, like black glass. She and the girl were the only things that had ever stepped into his heart. She and the girl and Old Smoky. The girl had stepped out again of her own volition, though the bright ghost of her remained.

But horses and mountains—they are the things that a man can count on. Whatever love you give them, they give back, as a mirror by the nature which God bestowed on it must return all the light that falls on its face. If his life were not at an end, if he had a new start to make with two good hands, he would do things differently. But that—well, that was all gone—everything was finished.

So he rubbed the soft muzzle of the mare in farewell.

He spoke a few foolish words over her, then walked into Rafferty's.

Rafferty was not there. No one was in the barroom. It was empty. Empty as a coffin, say, with only the bright image of the bottles in the mirror behind the bar. He walked heavily to the bar. Rafferty came in from the back room, wiping a brightness of grease from around his mouth. He was still chewing, but his jaws stopped working as he looked at Cheyenne.

"You, eh?" he said.

"How are you, Jim?" asked Cheyenne, with that smile of his.

"Well, I'll be damned!" said Rafferty.

He came hastily around the bar and faced Cheyenne. His big jowls trembled with excitement.

"You know what town you're in?" asked Rafferty.

"Good old Martindale, eh?"

"Well, I'll be damned!" said Rafferty again.

"I hope not," said Cheyenne. "Let's have a beer."

"A beer?" muttered Rafferty. He drew one, ruled off the fine bubbles of the excess head. "You have your beer, but I'll take a whiskey. I need it."

He threw off his drink, filled his glass again, and emptied it the second time. Then he resumed his study of Cheyenne.

"This here bunk they been telling me," said Rafferty. "About,"—he waved his hand—"about Crooked Foot . . . about Slip Martin . . . what's there in that?"

"Slip Martin?"

"You know what's being said?"

"That I took water from Slip?"

"By God, that's what they're saying, son. Knock me dead if that ain't what they're saying."

"Jim, you've been here long enough to remember Danny Martin."

"I knew the two-faced twicer," agreed Rafferty.

"You remember that he and Chuck Martin jumped me, one night?"

"I remember the night, all right. I remember where

Danny dropped dead . . . yonder . . . right in that corner."

"You're going to see another Martin die tonight, I think," said Cheyenne. "Mind inviting him in?"

"Who?"

"Slip Martin. Is he in town?"

"Yeah! Where would he be except swelling around this town, drinking the free drinks. You want him here? You mean it?"

"Not if he's drunk," said Cheyenne. "If he's sober, tell him that I'm waiting in here for him. Tell the other Martins, too."

Rafferty tore off his bar apron. "I been sick at the stomach ever since I heard about Crooked Foot," he said. "Cheyenne, what you say makes me feel like a man again. I'll get Slip. I'll get everybody. Leave it to me! And I'll frame your getaway, afterward! There ain't gonna be no murder on top of this here fair fight!"

Chapter Eleven
Doctor Lindus

Earlier that same night, Dorothy Martin has slipped out of her father's house by the side door. She went around through the corral and got hold of her bay mare. All the others scattered at her coming, stampeding into a far corner, where they swirled like currents of conflicting water for a time, then poured out again in a wild stream to either side.

The kitchen door opened. The loud, angry voice of her father bawled into the night: "What in hell's wrong with those horses? Steady, boys!"

But her father was not likely to come out to investigate because he had with him, tonight, the very head and topmost authority of the Martin clan—old Jefferson Martin, who ruled his community like a king. His authority was much reinforced, just now, because of the glory that had come to Slip Martin, his son.

Dorothy led her mare by the mane, carrying her pack slung over her shoulder. When she came to the shed, she did not venture to light a lantern. What she wanted, she could find. Her saddle always hung on the third peg from the door. She found it and swung it over the back of the bay. Usually she got one of the men to cinch up the girths tight. She did it herself tonight, patiently waiting for the bay to let out some of the air with which she swelled her chest against the pressure of the cinches. When she had the girths drawn up, she got the bridle on easily, the good mare opening her mouth and reaching for the bit as though she liked it.

There would be a frightful commotion when they

found her note. There would be a still greater excitement when she returned. Perhaps her reputation would be gone after that single excursion into the wilderness. A breath can sully a mirror and a word can destroy a girl. She had thought of all that before she started from the house. She had added up facts and feelings, and she faced the cold of the future steadily and without fear.

Now that the mare was ready, she started toward the door, pulling the horse after her in the direction of that dim speckling of starlight. But the mare, pulling sidewise on the bridle, bumped against the open door. The flimsy wood sounded like a stricken drumhead, and the whole mass of horses in the corral began snorting and racing again.

As she lifted her foot to the left stirrup, she could hear the stamping feet of men and their raised voices inside the house. The kitchen door flung open again and her father strode out, swearing, a rifle in his hands.

"There's some damn coyote around here," he said, "and I'm going to settle it. Don't go and disturb yourself, Jefferson." Then he shouted: "You there! You on that horse . . . hold still or I'll drill you clean, by God!"

She checked up the mare with a gasp.

"Get down off that horse and stick your hands up and come walking to me, dead slow!" shouted Ned Martin.

"Father!" said the girl. "It's only I. . . ."

"Hey, now what in thunder?" he demanded. "What are you doing out there at this time of night . . . ?"

"I'm only going for a jog down the road," she said. "I'll be right back."

"Stop that horse!" he shouted after her.

She reined in again. Such a weakness came over her that she began to tremble. Now the tall silhouette of her father bore down on her.

"You're going to jog down the road, this time of night, after dark? Dolly, what in thunder is in your head? What's the matter with you? What's *been* the matter with you, these last days? Get off that horse!"

She slipped to the ground.

"Nothing's the matter," she said. "Only, I wanted to get out alone for a few minutes."

"What's tied on behind that saddle?"

His hands fumbled there. Afterward he faced her in the darkness, and she heard him breathe once or twice before his voice came.

"Dolly, you've tied a pack on behind the saddle. You were going some place."

She did not need a light to see the pain in his work-starved face. The years of his tenderness and his love poured sorrowfully over her.

"I was going away for two days," she said.

There was another pause.

"Going away? For two days, Dolly?" he asked her. "Where?"

"I don't want to tell you."

"Would you mind coming back into the house?" said Ned Martin.

She wondered why his broken voice did not bring the tears into her eyes; but there was a deeper sorrow in her heart, a coldness of misery which had lain there for days. She walked back silently beside that tall, long-striding form. She was thinking of her childhood and her big father coming in from the cold and the wet of a winter night, with the steam of his breath blowing over his shoulders. She was remembering, strangely enough above all, her first struggle with algebra, and how his huge hand had cramped itself small to hold the pencil as he labored beside her, not helping but at least suffering with her, as he made his figures fine and small, like copy-book writing almost.

They went through the kitchen. The Chinaman grinned and bobbed his head at her. Chinamen never understand anything except how to be kind, she reflected. And that's the lesson which the world needs most.

They went into the dining room, one end of which was usually the family living room, also. There, by the cold stove, sat "Uncle" Jefferson, the father of Slip. Because of his fatherhood, the girl could not look at him squarely.

"Jefferson," said Ned Martin, "looks as though my girl was about to take a trip away from home. I thought that maybe you could reason with her."

How strange that her father should ask Jefferson Martin to "reason" with her! He, the father of Slip!

"What kind of a trip away? Where you goin', honey?" asked Jefferson Martin. He was a mountain. Time had worn away some of the sloping flesh, but the rocky frame remained, immense and awe-inspiring.

People said that he could be a savage when he was angry. But she looked into his craggy face without the slightest feeling of apprehension. Such blows had fallen on her, silently, that no words of Jefferson Martin could add to her burden.

"I can't say where I'm going," said the girl. "It would only make unhappiness."

"Ned," said Jefferson, "looks like you gotta bear down a mite on that gal."

Ned Martin reached out his bony hand toward Dorothy, then smiled, and shook his head. "How would I bear down on Dolly?" he asked.

"By the ripping thunder!" shouted Jefferson, his wrath flowing suddenly as he smote the edge of the table, "I'd give her a command and I'd see that she yipped out an answer! Dolly, where you planning to go?"

She said nothing. She merely watched his face curiously, fearlessly. Other people knew nothing about pain. How could they know?

"By God, Ned," said Jefferson Martin, "if it was a brat of mine, I'd up and lambaste her, is what I'd do. She ain't too old for it. If she was, I'd make her younger, a damn sight! Stand there and look you in the eye and say nothing, will she?"

The hoofs of horses and the light rattling of wheels drew up in front of the house. In the silence, during which Ned Martin sorrowfully examined his refractory child, there came a knocking at the kitchen door. The Chinaman opened it. He never could learn to ask questions. Every inquirer, even the most ragged tramp, was instantly brought by Wong into the heart of the family. So Ned Martin strode hastily to block away this interruption. But he was too late. Already the stranger stood in the dining room doorway.

Ordinarily, all that one sees at the first glance is eyes and mouth and nose; but what the girl saw in this stranger was a forehead so high and so wide, that it gave his face a bald look. The eyes glimmered rather vaguely behind thick glasses, and the lower part of his face was refined almost to femininity. His hands were pale and thin. He could be no hand on a ranch. But he had stamped on him an air of authority which would have made him pass as current coin—and gold at that—in any society.

"I've been looking for Mister Jefferson Martin," he said, "and I was informed that I could find him here. I am Doctor Walter Lindus, from Martindale."

"Hello, Doctor Lindus," said Jefferson Martin, getting to his feet. "I've heard tell of you. I've heard fine things told of you. It's a happy day for Martindale to have a doc like you in our town."

They shook hands. The introductions went round and, when the doctor shook hands with the girl, she felt his glance linger on her a little, as though in surprise. They were inviting this distinguished guest to sit down; they were assuring him that dinner would be on the table in a few moments. He cut straight through this hospitality.

"I can't stay," he said, "because I have to turn back immediately. I'll have to wear out my team, as it is, and drive practically all night. I simply have five minutes' talk on hand for you, Mister Martin."

"We'll step into Ned's front room," suggested Jefferson Martin.

"I can say it here just as well," said the doctor. "I'd rather speak with more witnesses, in fact. I've come over here because I've heard of the damnable outrage your son committed, Mister Martin!"

This sudden stroke, a blow in the face, caused the big

rancher not to recoil or straighten, but to lean a little forward with a darkening brow.

The doctor was not deterred by this attitude of Jefferson Martin. He went straight on, with that wonderful air of a man who is in control. He said: "Murder is a horrible crime, Mister Martin. But there are worse things, it appears. Your son has been guilty of one of them. He has taken advantage, publicly, of a helpless man. I refer to his cowardly behavior in a saloon in the town of Crooked Foot."

"Coward? Him a coward? My Slip a coward?" shouted Jefferson Martin, getting his voice up by degrees to a roar. "You mean my Slip . . . a coward? Him that faced down that man-murderin' Cheyenne? What kind of fool talk are you makin'?"

The doctor lowered his head a little. The highlight danced slowly on the big, bald knobs of his forehead. All that the girl could feel about him was brain, brain, brain. He was a man who knew, and whose knowledge could not be wrong. And suddenly a wild hope had come up in her heart and was pouring out toward him, clinging to him and his next words.

He was actually shaking his finger at Jefferson Martin. "You mean to say," he was exclaiming, "that you didn't know that poor Cheyenne is a helpless man? You mean to declare to me that you and all your tribe didn't know?" The doctor looked his disbelief. "I've been hunting for you," he said, "because I was told that you're in control of your clan. You mean to tell me, Jefferson Martin, that all of you are not perfectly aware that the right arm of Cheyenne is no better than half paralyzed?"

A dreadful stroke came in the throat and in the heart of Dolly Martin and beat her right down to her knees.

"What would you mean by that?" demanded Jefferson Martin. But the assurance was gone from him, now. "Paralyzed?"

"But, of course, you know all about it!" exclaimed the doctor. And he lifted his head, suddenly, and stared around him with a fine contempt for them all. "The eye-witness who told me about the thing distinctly described the holster that Cheyenne wore as being on his left hip. You must have been told the same thing. And your scoundrel of a son, sir . . . do you hear me? . . . I say that your coward of a son took a shameful advantage over a defenseless man whose spirit may have been broken forever, for all I know. And I am here to warn you Martins, individually and as a clan, that if a single finger is ever lifted against him in the future, I shall make it my business to publish the shameless facts all over this range!"

There was no question that the doctor held them all, easily, in the palm of his hand; and the girl began to get back on her feet.

"Cheyenne!" she said to the doctor. "Do you mean that he'll never be well again? Do you mean that his right hand will never be good again?"

"He has one chance in three . . . or in ten," said Walter Lindus.

"I knew he had a need of me!" cried Dolly Martin. "That was why I was starting to go to him tonight. There was a voice in my heart that told me to go. . . ."

Her father, at this, turned as pale as a blanched stone. But before another word could be spoken, the kitchen door was dashed open and the voice of Sanders, one of the hired cowpunchers, roared out in the next room: "Wong, gimme a hunk of cheese and a lump of bread. No supper for me. Ted Nolan's gone by with the word that Cheyenne is in Rafferty's place! Cheyenne is there . . . waiting for Slip Martin to come. My God, think what a fight it'll be! Cheyenne ain't a yellow dog after all, it looks like. He's right there in Rafferty's, now. Gimme that bread and cheese. I'm gonna get goin'. It'll be the greatest fight that ever was! It's a *duel*, Wong!"

Doctor Lindus was struck aghast. "Cheyenne waiting? Cheyenne challenging Slip Martin? Cheyenne standing up to a normal man? He's mad!"

"No, no," cried the girl. "Not mad . . . but he'd rather

die like a normal man than live to be shamed. And here we stand . . . while he's being murdered!"

She went swerving past her father and raced through the kitchen and outside. The door creaked slowly back behind her and struck with a heavy bang.

Chapter Twelve
The Great Heart

Martindale converged on Rafferty's saloon. Not all of Martindale, for the women and the children remained at home, of course, and they formed the whispering chorus against which the tragedy was to be enacted. The men headed for Rafferty's saloon, quickly, in steady streams.

Rafferty had found Slip Martin in a lunch room, eating pork chops and sauerkraut and French fried potatoes. Slip was washing down a mouthful with a good swallow of coffee and hot milk when the barman came in. He kept the cup at his mouth for a moment while his eyes dwelt on the face of Rafferty.

In that moment his mind jumped like a running rabbit through many ideas. The whole affair up there in the cabin on the side of Old Smoky had been a lead-on and the affair in the saloon at Crooked Foot had been a fake. These affairs were to draw him on for a killing—because nobody would blame Cheyenne if he killed Slip Martin, now. No, everyone would praise him.

And yet that business of managing the fork in the right hand, that surely had not been faked. The wobble of the fork, held like a dagger—that was not playacting! Perhaps like a beaten champion, the injured Cheyenne could not resist one more call to the ring. Well, this time Slip would kill him. This time Slip would put him down and out forever.

Rafferty left the lunch room, and a murmur began to spread up and down the street. The murmur would grow into shouting, later on, when Cheyenne was dead.

And Slip Martin went on with his meal, slowly. People

Max Brand

would talk about that, later. They would tell how Slip
Martin received the news about Cheyenne, and calmly
finished his meal, then went out and killed Cheyenne like
nothing at all. It isn't what a man does so much as the
way he does it. The style is the thing.

His meal done, Slip made a cigarette. He felt fine. He
went out across the dark of the street and around the
back way, then looked into the side window of Rafferty's
place. He saw the whole room filled with people. They
were plastered up against the bar and they were pooled
against the side wall, but no one stood near the end wall,
opposite the swing-door, for Cheyenne sat there at a
small table, sipping a glass of beer. Cheyenne was turned
a little to the left, in his chair. And Slip Martin saw now
that the holster was on his left hip.

Therefore Cheyenne was a dead man! Slip Martin,
grinning, went on studying details. He saw the beer glass
raised in the right hand of Cheyenne. The glass wobbled.
Cheyenne dipped his head a bit to meet the drink.

Slip could not help laughing. If he had been privileged
to set the stage, he would have put no other people on it.
Everyone in front of whom he wanted to appear great
was there. Everyone, that is, except Dolly Martin. But a
man can't have the world with a fence around it.

Slip turned away and rounded the front corner of the
building. Against the darkness he could still see the image of Cheyenne's handsome face, perfectly calm, with a
faint smile carved about the mouth. The man was brave.
If only those people inside could *know* how brave he was!

Slip pushed open the swing-door and stepped inside.
It was so easy that he could not help smiling. There was
no hurry. He could beat any left-handed draw by half a
second; and he could not miss a target that was only ten
steps away. He would reduce that distance to make sure.

But, as he took one stride forward, Cheyenne said:
"Stand fast!"

Cheyenne was rising, and Slip halted. At the authority
in that voice, something stopped in his heart. For Cheyenne spoke like one who cannot fail, who must be right.

144

Slip was still smiling. When he had both hands at his service, who in all the world would be fool enough to go up against this great champion?

He could not believe his ears—he could not believe that the deep, calm voice of Cheyenne was saying: "Friends, this fellow called me a yellow dog once. I've been trying to keep that down, but it won't stay. Slip, I'm going to do my best to kill you. Fill your hand!"

What made this man so calm, so sure that he offered the first move to an enemy? Had he managed to conjure into his left hand all the skill that had once resided in the right?

He stood tall and easy, close against the end wall of the room. His quiet smile had, surely, both disdain and surety in it. And the courage in Slip Martin rushed out of him, suddenly. He wanted to run. He knew that if he did not act quickly, he would flee. His own garb of hero was being torn to pieces, and his fear could be seen by everyone through the rents.

He screeched out in a queer, womanish voice: "Then take it, damn you!"

His gun was out as he yelled. But he triggered too rapidly. The first bullet ripped a long furrow down the flooring. The second was wide to the right. He was shaking. He could never hit his mark. And then he saw that the gun of that smiling, tall, handsome man was only now, gradually, leaving the holster. Left-handed? Cheyenne might as well have been trying to use the gun with his foot! That was why the third bullet from Slip's rapidly firing gun tore through the left thigh of Cheyenne.

Low, and too far to the left—even so, the man should have gone down. But he did not fall. His wide shoulders were pressed back against the wall, and his gun was tipping smoothly forward out of its holster.

Higher this time, thought Slip Martin, and more to the right. One more slug, properly placed, would fix Cheyenne for all time. The fourth bullet, more truly aimed, crashed straight into the body of Cheyenne.

Why didn't he fall? Why didn't he crumple, or pitch

forward, or slump weakly to the side? No, the wall upheld him—and the fourth bullet had only drilled through his right shoulder. And with the wall supporting him, as a screech of horror came from the throats of all who saw this smiling giant, slow of movement, endure without reply the fusillade from the weapon of Slip—now, as that yell began, and as the fourth bullet drove home, Cheyenne fired.

The bullet jerked the gun out of Slip's right hand and flung it back into his face. The impact knocked across his eyes a cloud of darkness mixed with sparks of shooting fire.

He was on his knees when his vision cleared. Blood streamed down his face from a rent in his forehead. And through the whirling mist he saw not the body of Cheyenne, still erect, but only the stony, smiling face, and the poised revolver.

"Don't shoot!" screamed Slip Martin. He wallowed on his knees in an agony. All of life that was about to leave him, imprinted its sweetness on his lips. The taste of it made him shriek again: "Don't kill me, Cheyenne. I'll tell 'em I was a yellow dog. I'll tell 'em how I knew your right hand was no good. Don't murder me, Cheyenne. I give up. . . ."

He began to crawl toward the swing-door, and the gun of Cheyenne did not explode. Slip leaped to his feet and fled. The impact against the swing-door let him escape, staggering, into the open might. And he ran for his life, with the blood from his forehead blinding him.

Inside the saloon, Cheyenne was saying: "You fellows have chalked Danny Martin up against me. I give you Slip, for an exchange. Does that make us square?"

He had no answer to this. For the Martins, with sick faces, were pouring out of the saloon into the open. So he got hold of the chair from which he had just risen, and lowered himself into it. The warmth of his blood was flowing all over his body and streaming down on the floor. Numb agony wakened momentarily into living pain.

Yellow Dog

He picked up his beer glass and drank off what remained in it, tipping his head back slowly. That was what Dolly Martin saw as she sprang through the doorway. She saw big Rafferty, like a portrait in stone, leaning paralyzed over his bar; she saw the crimsoned clothes of the wounded man, and the beer glass tilting at his lips.

Jefferson Martin and Ned strode in beside her. But she was the first to reach Cheyenne.

He said: "Dolly, things are all right. I'm only winged in a couple of spots. Don't look like murder . . . there's nothing very wrong. Only, the old left was pretty slow."

They laid him out on the bar. The blood ran down onto Rafferty's floor and into his wash sink, as they cut away clothes and got at the wounds to stop the bleeding. And as they got off his shirt, the letter came with it, half soaked in crimson.

"The Martins have no use for cowards." Then Cheyenne was adding, faintly: "Leave that with me. It's the reason I had to come."

"I wrote it, Dolly," admitted her father, with a wretched face. "When I saw the writing of a stranger on an envelope, I looked inside. And I couldn't have you writing to Cheyenne . . . not after what you did that night of the dance. I was too scared."

She waved him away. Because what he had done was in the past and all that really counted was the present and a certain golden glory which, she knew, was to make the future.

"I didn't write it, John," she cried above Cheyenne. "I didn't do it. It wasn't mine! It isn't my handwriting!"

His eyes had been closing and glazing with pain and with weakness. Now he opened them and looked suddenly up at her with understanding. "I should have known," he said. "You'd write a bigger hand! You'd write a lot bigger hand!"

The buckboard of Dr. Walter Lindus, by the grace of chance, came through Martindale some time later, and it was Lindus who searched and bandaged the wounds of Cheyenne. It was he who said to the girl at Cheyenne's side: "I don't know. That wound in the right shoulder may counteract the effects of the old wound. Or it may make the effects worse, but after this, he's safe enough on this range. No man will ever take another chance against him, my dear girl."

"Dolly," said Cheyenne, "could you keep on caring for a one-handed man?"

She drew her breath in sharply, instead of letting it go out in words. He looked up into the blue of mountain lakes. He could keep on looking into them for miles and miles. He began to smile. The girl smiled back like an image reflected. They said nothing.

As this silence endured for a time, the doctor saw that it was full of a meaning greater than music or speech, so he withdrew softly from the room and went into Rafferty's kitchen. There he stood as one stunned, unheeding poor Mrs. Rafferty who was busily offering a chair, and a drink beside it. The doctor was seen to look down at his own pale, thin hands. Then he said a thing that the Raffertys never quite understood.

"The great heart," said the doctor. "Never the hand, but always the great heart!"

THE RETURN OF
FREE RANGE LANNING

Frederick Faust's first contribution to *Western Story Magazine* was the five-part serial, "Jerry Peyton's Notched Inheritance," which began in installments under the byline George Owen Baxter in the issue for November 25, 1920. It was followed by two short novels, and then came the eight-part serial, "Iron Dust," again under the George Owen Baxter byline, beginning in the issue for January 15, 1921. "Iron Dust" is the story of a young blacksmith, Andrew Lanning, who is goaded into a fight with the town bully. Believing he has killed the man, Lanning takes flight and is pursued by a posse led by trigger-happy Bill Dozier. In an exchange of gunfire in defense of his own life, Lanning kills Dozier. A reward is offered for his capture, dead or alive, and Hal Dozier, a deputy U.S. marshal and Bill Dozier's brother, relentlessly takes to Andy's trail. In the course of his flight, Andy meets and falls in love with Ann Withero. At the end of the serial, having made Hal Dozier his friend, Andy is planning to mount his horse, Sally, and find Ann. The serial proved so popular with readers that that same year Street & Smith cut it from 84,000 to 64,000 words and issued it in book form as *Free Range Lanning* (Chelsea House, 1921). In "The Roundup" in *Western Story Magazine* for the issue dated March 10, 1923 the editor, Frank Blackwell, related a conversation he had supposedly had with Baxter: " 'How about it, George?' we asked him. 'In that "Iron Dust" story, do they get married? Does the man go after the pony or the girl?' Well, we asked him so hard that he wrote a sequel to it. . . ." "When Iron Turns to Gold" appeared in the July 30, 1921 issue of *Western Story Magazine*. For the sake of continuity with the previous book, this short novel's title has now been changed. Although almost fourteen years separates Andrew Lanning's story from the setting for "Yellow Dog," the town where Lanning is first seen working as a blacksmith is named Martindale, and it is to Martindale that he returns.

151

Chapter One
The Prodigal's Return

Even though the slope was steep and broken and cut with boulders, Andrew Lanning let the reins hang slack and gave the mare her head. But, in spite of the difficulty of the course before her, Sally gave only half of her attention to it. She was mountain bred and mountain trained and, accordingly, she had that seventh sense in her dainty feet to which only mountain horses ever attain.

She knew a thousand little tricks. She knew that, when gravel began to slip beneath her, the thing to do was not to stop merely or to whirl and go back, but to spring like a cat to one side. For that small beginning might mean a landslide of no mean proportions. By that seventh sense on those small, black hoofs she understood the rocks; she sensed which of them were too slippery for acrobatics and which, for all their apparent smoothness, were so friable that she could get a toehold. She knew to a fraction of a degree what angle of a slope was practicable for a descent and, as for climbing, if she did not quite have the prowess of a mountain sheep, she had the same heart and the same calm scorn for heights. With this equipment it was no wonder that Sally went carelessly down the slope according to her own free will, sometimes walking, sometimes sitting back on her haunches and sliding, sometimes breaking into a beautiful free gallop when she came onto a comparatively level shoulder of the hill.

But, no matter how busy she was, from time to time Sally tossed up a head that had made the heart of many a horselover leap, and regarded the valley below her. It was a new country to Sally, and about strange things she was as curious, as pryingly inquisitive as a woman. Everything about Sally, indeed, was daintily feminine, from the nice accuracy with which she put down her feet to the big, gentle, intelligent eyes, and there was even something feminine in the way her pricking ears quivered back to listen when her master spoke.

When he said, at length, "Ah, Sally, there's where I fight my big fight and my last fight," she came to an abrupt halt and raised her head to look down into the shadowy heart of the valley. From here one could plainly see the little village of Martindale and every winding of its streets. For the mountain air was as clear as glass. Having surveyed it to her own content, she turned her head and regarded the master from a corner of her eye, as one who would say: "I've seen a hundred towns, better or worse than that one. What the deuce is there about it to interest you?" But Andrew Lanning nodded to her, and she tossed her head again and started on down the slope, with the same nervous, catlike placing of her feet. Plainly these two were closely in tune. He was among men very much what she was among horses, with the same clean-cut, sinewy, tapering limbs and the same proud lift of the head and the same clear, dark eyes.

But as they drew closer to the bottom of the valley, his face clouded more and more with thought. He even went the length of drawing his rifle from its case to examine its action, and then he tried his revolvers. Having looked to them, he was more at ease, as could be told by the way he settled back in the saddle, but still it was plain that he approached Martindale very much in doubt as to the reception which waited for him there.

As if to hasten the conclusion, the moment the hoofs of Sally touched the smooth trail which slid down the valley floor, he gathered her to a fast gallop. She came up on the bit in a flash, eager to stretch out at full speed and, under the iron restraint of his wrist, her neck bowed. There was no suggestion of daintiness about her now. She was all power, all flying speed, all mighty lungs and generous heart, and she rushed down the trail with that deceptively easy, long stride which only a blooded horse can have. But, even in the midst of her joyous gallop, the mind of the master guided and controlled her, not with the tug of the reins, but with a word, and at his voice she canted her head just a trifle to one side, in the beautiful way that horses have, and seemed to listen and read his mind and his heart.

"Not so fast, Sally," he was saying. "Not so fast, old girl. We're going into Martindale at full gallop, and we may go out again with twenty men and hosses on our heels. Well, that won't be anything new to us, eh?"

The wind had picked up a little whirl of dust before her; she cleared it from her nostrils with a snort and then came back to an easier gait, smooth as flowing water; her rider sat like a rock. And so they came to the outskirts of Martindale. It was one of those typical mountain towns, weather-stained, wind-racked, with the huddling houses that gave a comfortable promise of warmth in the winter snows and of cool shade in the summer. Andrew Lanning called Sally to a walk and went slowly along the main street.

If Martindale were awake, it only opened one eye at Andrew Lanning. There were no people at windows or on porches, so far as he could see, and very few sounds of life from the interiors of the shacks. The predominate sound was the dismal bellowing of a cow on a hillside pasture above the town, a disconsolate mother mourning for a son who had gone to make veal for the hungry. Not a particularly cheery welcome for Andrew Lanning, and his heart grew heavier with every step Sally took.

His manner had changed the moment he came between the two lines of houses that fenced him in. He sat bolt erect in the saddle, looking straight ahead of him, but his eyes had that curious, alert blankness of the pugilist who looks into your eyes and is nevertheless watching your hands. Andrew Lanning was watching, while he stared straight down the street, every window, every door, every yard that he passed and, when a little girl of nine or ten years came out on the porch of a shack, a quiver ran through the body of the rider before he saw that the newcomer was harmless. He turned squarely toward the child, whose great eyes were staring at the beauty of the horse. Andrew brought Sally to a halt.

"Hello, Judy," he called. "Have you forgotten me?"

"Oh, my! Oh, my land!" exclaimed Judy, clasping her hands after a grown-up fashion. "Oh, Andy, you did come back."

He chuckled, but his glance slipped up and down the street before he answered. "Don't they expect me?"

"Of course they don't."

"Didn't Hal Dozier tell 'em I was coming?"

"He did, but nobody believed it. My dad said. . . ." She stopped and choked back the next words.

He leaned a little from the saddle. "Judy, you ain't afraid of me?"

Her hands were clasped again. She came toward him with slow, dragging steps, as though her curiosity were gradually conquering her timidity, and all the while she peered into his face. Something approaching a smile began to grow on her lips. "Why, Andy, you ain't so much changed. You're most awful brown and you're thinner and you're older, but you ain't changed. I think you're even a lot nicer. Is this the hoss that everybody talks about all the time? Is this Sally?"

"This is Sally. Do you know where I got her?"

"Did you . . . did you . . . shoot somebody for her?"

His lips twitched. "A little boy gave her to me, Judy. What do you think of that?"

"I don't see how he could. I don't, really, Andy."

She stretched out her hand with the palm up—man's age-old way of approaching a horse—and tried to touch Sally's face. Under the smooth-flowing voice of Andy the mare tremblingly submitted and, discovering that the soft, little, brown hand of the girl did not harm, Sally began to sniff at it.

"I know what she wants!" said Judy delightedly. "She wants apples or something. Ain't that it? Oh, you beauty! Might I ride her sometime?"

"Maybe. But what was it your father said?"

A shade of trouble came in her face. "I don't believe a single thing they say about you, Andy!"

"Of course you don't. You and me are old friends, Judy. But what does your dad say?"

"He says that . . . that . . . inside a couple of days you'll shoot somebody or get shot. That ain't true, is it, Andy?"

"Who knows, Judy?" he asked slowly. "But I hope not."

He sent Sally down the street again with a touch of his heel, and then, remembering, he turned with a sudden smile and waved to the child. She brightened at once and waved after him. It comforted Andrew immensely to know that he had this one small ally in the town. Everything, it seemed, had changed except Judy. Little Judy had grown lanky; even her freckles were bigger; but, inside, Judy was the same.

However, the town was different; it was more drab and shrunken, more hopeless. His discontent grew as he approached his destination, Hal Dozier's office. Rounding the bend of the street, he came in sight of it, and he also came in sight of the "commercial" district of the town, namely, the hotel and store and the blacksmith shop. The hotel verandah, that social gathering place of the mountain towns, was filled with idlers. They stared at Andrew with casual interest, but when they saw the full beauty of Sally their interest quickened. A buzz went up and down the length of the verandah, and every man came to his feet. Andrew knew then that they had recognized him.

Every nerve in his right arm began to tingle, as though it possessed a life of its own, and that life was endangered, and every nerve in his body called on him to whip out his gun. But he checked the impulse and fought it down with a great effort. Not a gun had shown on the verandah. One man or two had stepped back through the door, to be sure, but otherwise each man remained rooted to his place.

Andrew rode on, deliberately turned his back on them, and dismounted in front of Dozier's little town office. The big Dozier ranch was far out of town among the hills, but

Hal, who acted as a Federal marshal, had written that he would be in town in his office. He rose with a brief, deep-throated shout at the sight of Andrew Lanning. Sally had been attempting to follow her master into the office, but the shout of the marshal drove her back. She slipped over to the window and cautiously put her head through the opening to overlook this interview and see that no harm came to her rider.

"I gave you up yesterday," said Hal Dozier as he wrung the hand of Andrew Lanning. "Gave you up complete. Did you get my letters . . . both of 'em?"

"I'll tell you why I waited for the second letter," said Andrew frankly. "I wanted to give you time to find out from the men around town how they would take my return. When you wrote in the second letter that you thought they'd give me a square deal and a chance to make good, I decided to come in. It wasn't that I distrusted you . . . not for a minute. I knew that you'd be better than your word. You've got the governor's pardon for me. That was the first big thing that gives me a chance to live like an honest man and hold up my head. But my job is to win back the trust of these people around here."

The marshal shook his head. "I know what you want to do. And when I wrote to you and told you that they were willing to give you a fighting chance, I meant what I said. Just that and no more. You see, Andy, these block-heads have it fixed in their brains that, if a man is a killer once, he's a killer forever. I've tried to point out to them that you never were a killer, that you killed just one man, and that you killed him under excusable conditions. It makes no difference. They think the fever is in you, and that it will break out in gun talk, sooner or later."

"They're probably right," said Lanning sadly.

"Eh?" asked the marshal.

"I mean it. Look here!"

He took the sheriff to the back window and pointed to the upstepping ranges of the mountains, ridge after ridge pouring into the pale blue sky.

"That's been my country for these past few years," said

Andrew softly. "I've been king of it. The law has fought me and I've fought the law. A hard fight, and a hard life, but a wonderful one. Do you know the kind of an appetite it gives you to eat in a house surrounded by people who know there's a price of ten thousand dollars on your head? Do you know what it is to sleep with one ear open? Do you know what it is to go hungry for days, with towns full of people and food in plain sight and easy reach, but fenced away from you with guns? It's hard, but there's a tang to a life like that. I say I've lived like a king. My gun was my passport. It was my coin. It paid my debts and my grudges. And now I've stepped out of my kingdom, Hal, and I've come down to this."

He gestured despairingly toward the front of the little room at the street beyond. "Martindale! A rotten place for a grown-up man. No, Hal, it's hard to make the change. I'm going to fight hard to make it. I'm going to fight like a demon to be an honest man and work for my living, but every night I'll dream about the mountains and the freedom. And that's why I say that maybe they're right. Maybe I'll break loose before long. I've gone without roping for a long time. Maybe I'll jump the first fence I find in my way and land on another gent's property, or his toes."

Hal Dozier listened to this speech with a frown. "Then go away from Martindale. You know there's one place where you'd be welcome, a place where nobody has heard of you."

Andrew Lanning changed color. "Have you heard from her?" he asked huskily.

"I have." He handed Andy a letter, and the latter unfolded it slowly, breathing hard. He found written in a swift, free hand:

I know he is up for a hard battle, but he'll win. He has too much true steel in him to lose any fight he really wants to win. Will you tell him that for me? And will you ask him to write?

Max Brand

"Well?" said Dozier, as Andrew handed back the letter. "Will you do it? Will you write to her?"

"When I've earned the right to." He wandered slowly toward the door.

"What are you going to do now?"

"I'm going to find out for myself. I'm going to learn if those gents yonder on the verandah want me to stay, or want me to go back to the mountains. They can have their way about it."

Hal Dozier attempted to stop him, but he brushed the restraint aside and walked slowly across the wide street toward the hotel. Dozier, thoughtfully rubbing his chin, looked after him, and Sally trotted after her master until she had reached his heels and then followed like a dog, reaching out and trying to catch the brim of the wide sombrero in her teeth. For Sally still kept a good deal of the colt in her makeup.

Chapter Two
"Merchant and Mischief"

That evening Hal Dozier sat long at his desk, writing. Now and then he stopped to think, or even rose and paced the room until new ideas came to him, and it was late when he had finished a letter that ran as follows:

Dear Miss Withero:

I'm keeping the promise I made you to give you the news, as soon as there was news to give. To start with there's the biggest and best kind of news. Andrew has come into town!

He came as big as life, and very much as you must remember him; a little thinner, I think, and a little sterner, compared to the old Andy we used to know about Martindale. He came on Sally, of course, and Sally, at least, hasn't changed. I used to hate that horse. It was Sally, you know, who ran my 'Gray Peter' to death. But she's such a beauty that I've forgiven her. She follows Andy about like a dog. If it weren't for her he'd die of loneliness, I know.

But to get back to important facts. When Andy came in I ran over things as clearly as I could, told him that the governor had pardoned him for the past and hoped well for his future. I advised him to accept your invitation to go East, and I promised to help him in any way that I could.

But he was stubborn as steel. Under his gentle

manner there's no end of metal. As for you, he refuses to even mention your name, far less write to you, because, he says, he hasn't earned the right to speak to you. As for going East and working out his life in a new country, he says that he loves these mountains, that he belongs here, that in the East he'd be a fish out of water, and that, if he isn't strong enough to work out his destiny in his own land and among his own people, he doesn't want to live at all. He said these things in such a way that I couldn't find answers. I told him that the people of Martindale were neutral and pretty suspicious. But they'd give him a chance.

Do you know what he did then?

He walked straight out of my office and went to the verandah of the hotel. Here a dozen or more men were sitting around, and Andy made them a speech. I wish you could have heard it, it was so straight from the shoulder. And I won't forget him standing up as straight as a soldier and looking them all in the eye. He has a hard look to meet, has Andrew, as you may know someday if you ever make him angry.

He told them in words of one syllable that he knew he'd led a bad life for the past two years. He didn't make any bones of it, and he didn't make any excuses. That isn't his way. After he got started he acknowledged that he'd lived as an outlaw. He said that he wanted to come back to Martindale, where he was born, and show the people of it that he could live as a sober, hard-working citizen. He said it was a bargain. As long as he roved around the mountains he was simply a burden, for he lived off the work of other people. If he was allowed to settle down peaceably in the town he would cease being a burden for any one to carry. It was up to them. If they wanted to get rid of him and didn't want him around, they had only to say the word and he would jump on the horse that was standing behind him and ride away and never come back—peacefully. But if they al-

The Return of Free Range Lanning

lowed him to stay he would do his best to be as law-abiding as the next one.

Then he waited for his answer, but there was no answer made! They sat like owls on stumps and stared at him. They were afraid to give him a cheer and tell him to stay, and they were afraid to tell him to get out of town. Andrew waited a minute or two, and then he turned on his heel and walked away with his head down.

I tried to cheer him up and told him that the people of the town were simply waiting to see if he meant what he said, and that, as soon as he showed them, they would be with him heart and soul. But he was too shrewd to believe me.

He went to his old blacksmith shop and opened it. Things were a little rusty, but pretty much as they had always been. He polished it up a bit and then sat down at the door to wait for work. But there's a new blacksmith shop in Martindale, now, and all the work that came in to town today drifted right past Andy's old shop. They turned and stared at him, but they didn't ask him to shoe their horses.

Tonight he went back to his uncle's old house. I went to see him there. The old shack has run down since Jasper Lanning's death, and I found Andrew pacing up and down in the dust, with the old, warped boards of the floor creaking under him. Not a very cheery place for him, you see. And he was as restless as a wolf in a cage, and every once in a while he would stop his pacing at a window and look out at the mountains and then begin to walk up and down again, leaving his trail in the dust of the floor.

He was in an ugly mood, but he tried to keep it concealed. He swore that he would stay on as long as he could, and then I came back to my office to write to you.

I'm afraid for Andy, Miss Withero, I'm mortally afraid. He's closer to me than anything on earth. I went to kill him for the sake of the price on his head.

Max Brand

He shot me down and then fought with four men to save my life. Men of Andy's stamp aren't turned out every day, and it's a pity to see him fail.

But fail he inevitably will. The men of this town are watching and waiting for an explosion, and the more they watch and the more suspicious they grow the more nervous Andrew is. He knows that a lot of them hate him and would shoot him in the back if they could. Sooner or later some one is sure to get drunk and cross him, or some crowd will get together and try to bully him. If either of these things happen, some one is going to die. It won't be Andrew. After the explosion he'll be on Sally on his way back to the mountains and the free life he loves. So you can very well see that I live over dry powder, with sparks flying all the time. When will Andy blow up?

There's one thing that can dampen the powder. There's one thing stronger than Andrew's nervousness. You know what that one thing is—his love for you. It's more than a love; it's worship. You're more than a woman to him. He's dressed you up as a saint, aureole and all. When he speaks of you his voice changes, and he lowers his eyes.

Well, Miss Withero, I think you would do a good deal to help Andrew. I want to find out how much. Will you come West to Martindale and see Andrew and give him patience for the fight? Five minutes of you mean more to him than five years of adventure and freedom.

He doesn't know that I've written to you. I don't dare tell him. He thinks he must make himself go through the trial and try to see you after he has proven himself. But I say that the trial is greater than his strength. What will you do?

Hal Dozier

The marshal wrote that letter in the best of good faith, never dreaming that out of that letter would come the hardest test young Andrew Lanning was ever to receive.

164

The Return of Free Range Lanning

Moreover, it was destined to enter many hands and put strange thoughts in many minds and bring great results, some of which the marshal hoped for and some of which were the opposite of his desires.

It began by interrupting an important conversation. The conversation in itself was the result of long planning on the part of Charles Merchant. For a month he had been laboring to bring about a meeting between himself and Anne Withero, and eventually he had been able to maneuver until he was invited to this weekend party at the house where Anne was a guest for the summer. It was a typical Long Island estate, with oceans of lawn washing away from a Tudor house, so cunningly overgrown with vines and artificially weathered that, though it was hardly ten years old, it looked five hundred. Beyond the lawns were bits of an ancient forest, though it was not quite so ancient as it looked. In one of these groves Charles Merchant would have greatly preferred to have the walk and talk. But the best he could do was to keep Anne strolling up and down in the formal garden, in full sight of the house, almost in hearing of the guests. It was one of those foolish little hand-made gardens, with hedges clipped and sculptured into true curves and rigid square edges and flower beds planned like a problem in geometry. Stiff benches, that no one in the world would ever dream of sitting on, added to the artificiality, and imported French sculptures of the seventeenth century, dotted here and there, ladies with fat legs and silly little grinning faces and simpering, corpulent cupids, completed the picture. It was one of those formal French gardens which call from every nook and cranny: "Man made me, and God had absolutely nothing to do with it!"

But from this garden one could look through graceful oaks, on the edge of the hill, down to the blue of the sea. Through those trees the glances of Anne Withero went; but the glances of Charles Merchant never strayed from the face of the girl. He could not tell exactly where he stood with her, but he felt that he was making very fair progress. In the first place, she was listening to him, and

165

that was really more than he had reason to hope. His argument was based on a very old doctrine.

"If I have done things that were wrong, and heaven knows I have, it was because I was fighting to keep you, Anne. And you know everything is fair in such a case, isn't that true?"

And she had answered: "To tell you the truth, Charlie, I'm trying to forget all about the mountains and what happened there. I'm trying to forget anything very bad that you may have done. Is that what you want to know?"

It was not all, and he was frank to tell her so. "If you succeed too well," he said, "you may forget me altogether. I'd rather be remembered a little, even if it has to be viciously!"

He was convinced that he was very far on the outskirts of her attention, and it cut him to the quick. Had she not once been his prospective wife? But he clung to the task, and before long she was listening with more attention, though she persisted in confining their walk to the ridiculous little paths of that garden. He grew bolder as the moments passed. When she asked him when he was going West he said: "When I have to give up hope."

"Just what do you mean by that?" she asked him, and she asked it so unemotionally, so far from either scorn or invitation, that he was abashed, but he said gravely: "I mean that I'm struggling to win back your friendly respect first, Anne. And when that comes . . . well, then I'll go on hoping for something else. Do you think I'm wrong to do so?"

He had always been a proud and downright fellow, and he knew that his humility was what was breaking down her dislike for him and opening her mind; but he was delighted beyond all bounds when she did not at once return a negative answer to his last question. Indeed, she did not answer at all and, when she straightened and looked wistfully at the rich blue of the sea beyond the yellow-green oaks, he knew that she was remembering pleasant things out of their mutual past. He had his share of intuition and cunning, and he discreetly kept silence.

The Return of Free Range Lanning

It was at this very moment that the letter was brought to her. She glanced down at it carelessly and continued her walk but, presently looking down again, she seemed to read the address and understand it for the first time. He saw her hand hastily cover the writing on the envelope, and at the same time her eyes became alert. She wanted to get rid of him at once, and he knew it. More than that, when she looked at him now there was a certain hardness in her eyes. Something about that handwriting had made her suddenly call up her old anger, her old distaste for him.

But still, though the test was a stern one, Charles Merchant was not a fool. He brought her back to the house at the first pretext and left her alone with the infernal letter; then he went to find Anne's maid.

When he had decided that life was not worthwhile without Anne Withero, and that he must make a deliberate and determined campaign to regain his old position with her, he had, like a good general, cast about to find a friend in the enemy's camp. By means of a small subsidy he had secured a friend in the person of Mary, Anne's maid. She had already proven invaluable to him in many ways. She could not only keep him informed of her mistress' movements, but she was also intelligent enough to catch the general drift of Anne's interests of the moment. When Anne was reading books of the West and talking about the mountains, Charles Merchant knew perfectly well that her mind was turning to Andrew Lanning, that strange adventurer who had literally dropped out of the sky to ruin his own romance with Anne Withero. And, when Anne read and talked of other things, Charles knew in turn that she was letting the memory of her outlaw lover grow dim. In time, and with three thousand miles between them, he was sure that the girl would forget the fellow entirely. Any other solution was socially impossible. But he remained uneasy.

He met Mary at their appointed rendezvous beyond the tennis courts, and he told her at once what he wanted.

"Your lady got a letter a few minutes ago," he said, "a

fat letter on blue-white paper. You know the cheap stuff and the big, sprawling handwriting. You can't mistake it. Now, I want that letter to be in my hands before the night comes, you understand?"

When Mary stood with her hands folded and her eyes cast down, there was a good deal of the angel in her pale face. When she glanced up quickly, however, one found a pronounced seasoning of mischief in her eyes. And now she looked up very quickly, indeed. In her heart Mary despised big, handsome Charles Merchant; she had her own opinion of men who could not take the queen of their hearts by storm, but had to resort to such tactics as bribing maids. Nevertheless, she had decided to serve Charles Merchant. It was really for her mistress' sake more than her own. For Charles Merchant was rich, and he was also weak. An ideal man for a master and, also, from Mary's point of view, for a husband. If Anne married him she, Mary, would retain a mighty hold on the purse and the respect of the master of the house. She might even stand at the balance between master and mistress of a great establishment. She would be the power behind the throne. All of these things were in her mind as she now looked into the face of Charles Merchant, but she could not keep back the small grimace of mockery.

"Mister Merchant," she said, "may I ask you just one thing?"

"Fire away, Mary."

"After you marry Miss Withero, will you keep on handling her the same way?"

He laughed, and there was a sigh of relief behind the laughter. "After we're married!" he exclaimed. "After we're married, I'll find a way of handling her, never doubt that. Plenty of ways."

There was something in his manner of saying this that made Mary's eyes grow very big, and a sudden doubt of Charles Merchant came to her. His short command for her to hurry sent her away before she had time to speak again, but she went away thoughtful.

Chapter Three
Baiting the Hook

That night the letter was in the hands of Charles Merchant. He read it hastily, for Mary was waiting anxiously to take it back to its proper place. He detained her for a moment.

"Has she been talking about anything unusual?" he asked almost fiercely.

"No, nothing."

"Thank goodness!" said Merchant. "You're sure? No mention of a journey?"

Mary grew thoughtful. "She asked me, when she was dressing for dinner, if I had ever been West, and if I'd like to go there."

Merchant groaned. "She said that?"

"What's in that? She was just talking about the mountains."

"Only the mountains?"

"And she said there was a different breed of men there, too."

"That's all!"

He slammed the door after her and, going back to the window, slumped into a chair with his face between his hands. For all that he shut out the light from his eyes, he was seeing too clearly the picture of the lithe fellow, straight, graceful, dark eyed, and light and nervous of hand that was Andrew Lanning. He cursed the picture and the name and the thought of the name, as his mind went back to the night, so long ago, when the figure had leaned over his bed and asked through the darkness: "Where is the girl's room?" And then, lest he make an

169

outcry and alarm the house, Lanning had tied and gagged him.

In truth, the coming of Lanning had tied and gagged him forever, so far as Anne Withero's interest was concerned. Afterward the name of Lanning had grown in importance, had become a legend, one of those soul-stirring legends that grow up, now and then, around the figure of a stirring man of action.

An outlaw certainly was beyond the pale of Anne's interest, but Charles could see now that, perhaps, the very strangeness of the wanderer's position and character had made him fascinating in the romantic eyes of the girl. And then, striking back through a thousand dangers and risking his life for the sake of one interview, Andy Lanning, the outlaw, had come to the Merchant house again and seen Anne Withero once more. Only twice they had seen one another, but out of those two meetings had come the wreck of his own affair with her. He gritted his teeth when he recalled it.

Moreover, he was quite certain that Hal Dozier was right. Hal was a shrewd judge of men and events. If he said that the girl could tame wild Lanning and keep him a law-abiding man, then he was right. But he must also be right when he said that Lanning was balancing on a precarious edge, ready to fall into violent action and outrage society again.

Was it not possible, then, to knock the ground from beneath the tottering figure? Could not the necessary impetus be supplied which would throw Lanning off his balance and plunge him once more into a career of crime? There must surely be a way. And he, Charles Merchant, had money, could buy whom he willed to buy. The cause was worth it! It was a crusade, this saving of such a girl as Anne Withero from the low entanglements of an ex-criminal.

He packed his things that night. In the morning he said good bye to her.

"I'm going West, Anne," he told her. "I see that the past is still too close to you, and that you haven't been able to forgive me entirely. I'm going West and wait, for I haven't given up. I'm going to come back and try again. In the meantime, if it should happen that you need a helper, let me know. Will you do that?"

Even then he hoped that she might confide enough in him to admit that she was soon going West herself, but he was disappointed. She gave him a chilly farewell and no hint of her plans. In the morning he returned to New York and purchased a ticket for the West. Then he bought an early edition of an evening paper and went into the smoking room of the station to wait for his train. His eyes took in the headlines dimly. How could print catch his attention when a story of far more vital interest was running through his mind?

He turned the page and a bulldog face caught his eye. He liked it for the ugliness that fitted in with his own mood of the moment. There was a consummate viciousness and cunning about the little eyes, protected under massive, beetling brows; there was power and endurance in the blocky chin; and the habitual scowl fascinated Merchant, for it was his own expression of the moment. He raised his hand and smoothed his forehead with grinding knuckles, and still the face held his eyes.

"Lefty Gruger," he read beneath the picture, "pardoned!"

It was placed in large letters—an event of importance, it seemed, was the pardoning of this Gruger. With awakened interest he followed the rather long article.

It developed that Lefty Gruger had been serving a life term on many counts. If he had lived to the age of two hundred, his term of punishment would still be unspent. But Lefty Gruger had been for eight years an ideal prisoner. Never once did the prison authorities have the slightest trouble with this formidable murderer for such, it seemed Lefty Gruger had been. The man had apparently reformed. The reporter quoted one of Lefty's quaint sayings: "I dunno what's in this heaven stuff, but maybe it ain't too late for me to take a fling at it."

In reality, during the eight years his life had been exemplary, he had never become a trusty on account of the appalling nature of the crimes attributed to him, but he was on the verge of this elevation when the outbreak came. It was one of those mad, unreasoning outbreaks that will come now and then in prisons. An unpopular guard was suddenly hemmed against the wall, and his weapons were torn from him by a dozen furious prisoners. He was already down and nearly dead when a small, but well-directed, tornado struck the murderers in the person of Lefty Gruger. He had come out of the blacksmith shop with the iron part of a pick in his hand and he went through the little host of assailants, smashing skulls like eggs as he went.

In the sequel the guard's life was saved, and seven prisoners died from the terrible effects of Lefty Gruger's blows. But this heroism could not go unnoticed or unrewarded. The governor examined the case, determined to give Lefty a chance, and forthwith signed a pardon which was pressed upon him. The result was that the governor's benign face appeared in a photograph beside the contorted scowl of Lefty Gruger. That was worth at least fifty thousand votes in certain parts of the state though it was pointed out, with grim smiles in the police department, that Gruger was freed from a life sentence because he had killed more men at one sitting than he had been condemned for in the first instance.

The major portion of the article had to do with the desperate heroism of Lefty Gruger to save the guard, then with a detail of his exemplary conduct while in prison, and finally there was a very brief resumé of Lefty's criminal career, now happily buried under the record of his more recent virtues. It seemed that Lefty had been a celebrated gunman for many years, that he had escaped detection so long because he always did his jobs without confederates, and that, although it had been long suspected that he was guilty of killings, it was not until he had served ten years of criminal life that he was finally taken and convicted.

Once in the hands of the law it turned out that there

were various people willing to inform against the professional murderer, men who had been held back by fear of him until he was safely lodged in the hands of the law. Now they were ready and eager to talk. Into the hands of the police came more or less convincing proof that Lefty Gruger had certainly been responsible for five murders, and perhaps many more. But even this testimony was not of the first order. The result was that, instead of hanging, Lefty received a life sentence.

Now he was returning to his old haunts off the Bowery. The street address drifted into Charles Merchant's mind hazily. He was thinking with dreamy eyes, building a fairy story in the future. That dream lasted so long that the train departed with no Charles Merchant on it. Then he rose and sauntered into the street and took a taxi to the Bowery. At the stand where he had his shoes polished, in the hope of hearing chance news, the word was dropped:

"Lefty's back. He's at Connor's."

Merchant, leaving his chair as the shine was completed, sauntered into a lunch counter across the street. Sitting at the end of the counter nearest the window, he kept a steady eye on the pavement and houses opposite. Still retaining that survey, he covertly counted out a hundred dollars in crisp bills and shoved them into a blank envelope.

Lefty Gruger was not long out of sight. Having become a hero overnight, he had to harvest the admiration of his fellows, and presently he was observed to stroll down the steps of his rooming house, preceded and surrounded by half a dozen hard-faced fellows as Merchant had ever seen. But, among them all, the broad, scowling face of Lefty stood forth. Every brutal passion found adequate expression in some line or corner of his face. Suddenly it seemed to Merchant that he had known the recesses of that dark mind for years and years, and he felt himself contaminated by the very thought. He scribbled a few words on the envelope and left the lunch counter hurriedly. Crossing the street, he managed to intercept the course of Lefty's crew at the far corner. He sidled apologetically through the midst of them and, passing Lefty, he shoved the envelope containing the money into the latter's coat pocket and went on.

Although he did not pause, it seemed to him that the stubby hand of Lefty had closed over that envelope, and the square-tipped fingers had sunk into the missive, and that he sensed the contents by their softness. But Merchant hurried on, took a taxi at the nearest corner, and went straight to a hotel. He had written on the envelope:

Inside two hours, at the corner of Forty-seventh and Broadway, east side of the street.

In the hotel he flung himself on the bed, but he could not rest.

Chapter Four
A Gunman's Creed

He knew very little about such matters, but he imagined that once a notorious criminal was at large the police must keep an eagle eye upon him. If Lefty came to that meeting place, there might very well be a whole corps of observers on the watch from hidden places, and they might follow Lefty and note the interview with Merchant. But then again it was very doubtful if Lefty would make his appearance at all. He had a hundred dollars in his pocket for which he need not make an accounting. There was only one thing to which Charles Merchant trusted and that was, having made such a little stake of easy money, the killer might continue on the trail.

He wasted the two hours which remained before him with difficulty, and then went out and took his place at the head of Times Square, in the full rush of the late afternoon crowd. Eagerly he swept the heads of the crowd, but there was no Lefty. Presently he felt a light jerk at his coat, and then a stocky little man hurried past him and shouldered skillfully through the mob. It was Gruger beyond a doubt. The rear view of those formidable square shoulders was almost as easily recognizable as the face of the criminal. Merchant followed unhesitatingly.

Gruger opened the door of a taxi waiting at the curb and stepped in, leaving the door open. Merchant accepted the silent invitation and climbed into the interior. The abrupt starting of the engine flung him back to the seat, and the driver reached out an arm of prodigious length and slammed the door. It seemed to Merchant that he was trapped and a prisoner. An edge of paper in his own pocket caught his eye as he looked down. He drew out his own envelope and saw, as it bulged open, the money. He shoved it into an inside coat pocket and then for the first time turned to Lefty. The latter wore a faint, ugly smile.

"But I intended this . . . ," began Merchant, oddly embarrassed.

"I know," said Lefty, "but I don't take coin till after I've done a job, and then I want spot cash."

There was something so formidable about the way he jerked out these words that it made Merchant feel as though the gunman had already done a killing and now demanded payment. He moistened his lips and watched the stocky little man.

"But I thought you might be in need of a little stake," he ventured again.

"I ain't never broke," declared Lefty in his positive manner. "I got friends, mister. Now what you want?"

"I want in the first place to go where we can talk."

"You do, eh? What's the matter with right here?"

"But the driver?"

"Say, he's right. He's a friend of mine."

"But suppose we were seen to have entered this cab and were followed?"

"Pal, nobody ain't going to follow him, not through this jam!"

The driver was weaving through the press of traffic with the easiest dexterity, seeming to make the car small to slip through tight holes, and keeping in touch with his motor as though it were a horse under curb and spur.

"In the first place," began Merchant heavily, "I don't know how to let you know that you can trust any promises I make in regard to. . . ."

"Money? Sure you can. You're Charles Merchant. You come out of the West, you got a big ranch from your old man, and your bank account would gag a mule. All right, I know you."

Charles Merchant swallowed. "How in the world . . . ?"

"Did I tumble to that gag? I'll tell you. You didn't think I let you do a fadeaway after you passed me the bunk, do you? Nope. I ditched the gang, done a side step and slid after you to your hotel, grabbed your name off the book, and the rest was easy."

"How?"

"How? Why I got friends. They looked you up inside half an hour, and there you are. Now what's what?"

There was something startling in this abrupt way of brushing through preliminaries and getting down to the heart of things. Merchant had expected long and delicate diplomatic fencing before he even broached the aim he had in mind. He found that he was brought to the heart of his subject inside the first minute.

"In a word," he said, breathing hard, "it is a task of the first magnitude."

Lefty studied him, not without contempt and just a touch of bewilderment.

"Guess I get you. Somebody to be bumped off? When and where, and what's the stake?"

Merchant gasped. Then he answered tersely: "As fast as you can get to the place. That place is Martindale, and it's a good two thousand miles from New York. The price is what you think it's worth."

"I don't like out-of-town jobs," said Lefty calmly. "They get me off my feed a little, and two thousand miles is pretty bad. Seeing it's you, ten thousand ain't too much to ask."

He said it in such a business-like manner that, although Merchant was staggered by the price, he did not seriously object. A moment's thought assured him that ten thousand was cheap, infinitely cheap, if it brought him to his goal.

"And when do you want me to start, governor?"

"At once. About the money, what part will you want?"

"Ain't I told you that I'm never broke? I don't need any."

"The whole thing after . . . after . . . ?"

"After I deliver the goods? That's it!"

"But how do you know . . . ?"

"That you'll pay? Easy! You think it over a minute and you'll see why you'll pay."

And Merchant knew with a shudder that this was the last debt in the world that he would try to dodge.

"Now that we've settled things," he said, "I want to tell you about the man in the case."

"He don't matter," said Lefty largely. "He don't matter at all. All I want is his name."

Charles Merchant rubbed his chin in thought. It was strange that sectional pride should crop out in him in this matter of all matters. He looked coldly upon Lefty Gruger.

"Ever have a run-in with a Western gunfighter?" he asked.

"Me? Sure. Went as far West as Kansas City once and got mixed up with a tough mug out of the hills. They told me he was quick as a flash at getting out his cannon. Bunk! A revolver is pretty fair, but an automatic is the medicine for these Western gunfighters! They shoot one slug, standing straight up. I spray 'em by just holding down my finger. Fast draw? I don't draw. I drop a fist in my pocket and let her go!"

"Was that how it went with the gunman you met in Kansas City?"

"Sure it was. The boob didn't have a chance. He stood up straight like a guy getting ready to make a speech and grabs for his gat. I jumps behind a table and begins zig-zagging. He didn't have a chance of hitting me. While I was jumping back and forth, I turn on the spray. Seven slugs, and they all landed. He wouldn't of held a pint of water he was so full of holes when I finished with him."

Charles Merchant wiped his forehead. What he had looked upon as a forlorn hope changed to a feeling of far greater certainty.

"Now," he said, "listen to reason. You may be very good with a gun. Of course you are. But this fellow, Lanning. . . ."

"First name?"

"Andrew! This Andrew Lanning is good with a gun, too.

The Return of Free Range Lanning

He's beaten the best men of the mountains. With rifle or revolver it doesn't seem that he can miss. You may be almost as good but, if you stand up to him, you stand a fine chance of being killed, Lefty. Don't take the chance. Make a sure thing of it!"

"Shoot him in the back?" said Lefty coldly. "That what you mean?"

"Why not? You'll get ten thousand just the same!"

The voice of Lefty changed to a snarl. "Maybe you think," he said furiously, "that you're talking to a butcher? Maybe you think that?"

"I . . . I . . . ," Merchant choked in his distress. "The fact is, in a business like this, I like to feel that my money is invested as safely as possible, and I think. . . ."

"I want you to think this!" said Lefty, and he shook a swiftly vibrating forefinger under the nose of his companion. "You're talking to a white man. I never shot a gent while he had his back turned. I never shot him when he was took by surprise. I never shot him when he was drunk. I never shot him when he was sick. I've fought every man face to face. They flopped because they didn't have the nerve or the dope on gunfighting. That's my way. If a bird is good enough to flop me, then he collects, and I don't. That's all. If I didn't work for my coin, d'you think I could enjoy making it? No! I ain't a mankiller, I'm a sportsman, mister, and you want to write it down in red. Gimme a good sporting chance and I take it. Give me a sure thing and I tell you to go hang. I've never took up a sure thing, and I never will. But I'm after game, big game! Some gents like to go out into the jungle and hunt for tigers. I have more fun than that because I hunt things a thousand times worse'n tigers. I hunt men. It ain't the money alone that I work for. I got enough salted away to do for me. But I like the fun, bo. It's in my nature."

He sat back again, contented, flushed after having expounded his creed, defying Merchant to argue further in the matter. It bewildered Charles, this singular profession of faith.

"This Lanning guy . . . ?" went on Lefty more gently.

"You stop worrying. I'll plant him. I'll salt him away with lead so's you never have to worry about him none no more. That what you want?"

When Charles Merchant nodded, the gunman continued easily. "You just jot down the directions to the place. That's all I want."

Chapter Five
Concerning Sally

From the roof to the bellows there had been hardly a thing about the old blacksmith shop that did not need repairing. The anvil alone was intact. Even the sledge hammers were sadly rusted. He spent the first few days putting things in order and making repairs. But this was about the only work that came his way. To be sure, now and then, some one of the more curious dropped into his shop and had a horse shod in order to see the celebrated desperado at work. It would be something to ride home and point to the iron on the feet of a horse and say: "Andrew Lanning put those shoes on. I seen him do it."

But this made up a mere dribble of work, though Hal Dozier had sent in a few small commissions from his ranch. He had even offered to set up a shop for Andy on his ranch and said that he had ample ironwork to remunerate both himself and Andrew, but the ex-outlaw had other plans. He was determined to fight out the battle in Martindale itself.

There was something dreamlike about the whole thing. It had not been so many years ago since the men of Martindale looked down on the "Lanning kid" as being "yaller clear through." In those days they had greeted any mention of his name with a smile and a shrug. Then came the unlucky day when he knocked down a man and fled in fear of his life, leaving an unconscious victim who appeared to be dead. Feeling that he was outlawed by his crime, Andy had become an outlaw in fact. That was the small, the accidental beginning which, it seemed, was to determine the whole course of his life. He had plenty of chances to think about himself, past and future, as he sat idly in the little shop, day after day, waiting for work.

His funds were dwindling meanwhile. An angle of the affair, at which he had not looked before, now presented itself. He might be actually starved out of the town. He might be starved into submission.

All day, every day, he could hear the cheery clangor of hammer on anvil in the new and rival blacksmith shop down the street. There was plenty of business there, plenty of it! His competitor had tried to placate this terrible rival soon after his arrival. He came to visit the latter in his shop at the beginning of the working day.

"I'm Sloan," he said, "Bill Sloan. Maybe you don't know me?"

"Sure," said Andy. "I know you."

"You and me being sort of business rivals, as you might say," said Sloan, "I got this to say for a start. I ain't going to use no crooked ways of getting customers away from you, Lanning."

"I guess you won't," said Andrew gently.

"Matter of fact, now and then, I get an overflow of trade. I might send some of it down to your shop, Lanning."

It touched Andrew, the embarrassment of this huge, sturdy-hearted fellow. He went to him and touched his shoulder.

"Sloan," he said, "I know what's on your mind. You think I'm getting mad at you because you get the work. I'm not. Get everything you can and don't send me any overflow. You're married and you have kids. Get all the work you can. As for me I'm not going to try to rustle trade with a gun."

On the afternoon of the next day Hal Dozier stopped before the shop with a suggestion.

"Andy," he said, "Si Hulan is in town. Staying up at the hotel right now. He's looking for hands. Why don't you trot up to see him? He'd be glad to take you on if he has any sense. Got a big ranch. Soon as he learns that he can trust you, he'd be apt to make you foreman. You're the man to handle that rough gang of his."

Andy Lanning was not at all enthusiastic.

"You see," he replied, "I'd be glad to do that, but Sally isn't much good at working cows. She's never had much experience."

"You could teach her."

"I could teach her, but that dodging and hustling around in a bunch isn't very good for a hoss' legs."

"I know. Then ride another horse, Andy. Keep Sally for Sundays and holidays, eh?"

"Ride another hoss?" asked Andrew. "Man alive, Hal, you don't mean that!"

"Why not?" asked the marshal.

Andrew was breathless. "Sally and me," he attempted to explain. "Why . . . Sally and me are pals, you might say, Dozier."

He whistled softly, and at once the lovely head of Sally came around the corner of the shop. There she stood with her head raised, then canted to one side, her ears pricked, while she examined her master curiously.

"She plays out there all day," said Andrew, smiling at the mare. "I turn her loose in the morning when I come down to work, and she follows down here and plays around in the lot. Sometimes old Mrs. Calkin's dog, old Fanny, you know, comes over and plays a game with Sally. Game seems to be for Fanny to set her teeth in Sally's nose, and for Sally to let her come as close to it as she can without doing it. Hear Sally snorting and Fanny snarling and you'd think they was a real battle on. Well, you see how it is. I couldn't very well get on with Sally if I rode another hoss. Besides, the minute I got off another hoss, Sally would kick the daylights out of the nag. That's Sally's way, jealous as a cat and ready to fight for attention. She'll come over here and nose in between us pretty soon if I talk to you and don't pay no attention to her."

He rose as he spoke and winked at the marshal. "Watch her now!"

He turned his back on Sally, and the marshal looked

from one to the other of them. He thought them very much alike, these two. There was the same touch of wildness in both, the same high-headed pride, the same finely tempered muscles, the same stout spirit. Only one man had ever succeeded in riding Sally with a saddle, and that man was her present master. For the rest she was as wild as ever. And it came to the marshal that the same was true of the boy. One person in the world could tame him, and that was Anne Withero.

Sally had stood her exclusion from the conversation as long as possible. She now snorted and stamped with a dainty forefoot. It caused Andy to wink at the marshal, but he gave her no direct attention and, presently, she came hesitantly forward and, in reach of Andy, she laid her short ears back on her neck and bared her teeth. The marshal stifled an exclamation, so wicked was the look of Sally at that moment, so snakelike she was with her long, graceful neck and glittering eyes. The teeth closed on a fold of Andy's shirt at the shoulder, and she tugged him rudely around.

He faced her with pretended anger. "What kind of manners is this?" demanded the master. "You need teaching, and, by hell, you'll get it. Now get out!"

He threw up his arm, and the horse sprang sideways and back, lithe and neat footed as an enormous cat. There she stood alert, with ears pricking again.

"Look at that," said Andy. "Ready for a game, you see? What can you do with a hoss like that?"

"Ain't you ever had to discipline her? Never used a whip on her?" asked the marshal.

"I should say not!" replied Andy. "If I seen a gent raise a whip on Sally, I'd. . . ."

"Wait a minute!"

Andy shuddered and allowed the interruption to silence him. "I dunno," he muttered. "I could stand almost anything but that. If they was to shy a stone at Sally, like they done the other day. . . ."

"Did they do that?" asked the marshal softly.

"It was the Perkins kid," said Andy. "Sally dodged the

stone a mile, but it was sharp edged enough to have hurt her bad. I went in to see Jim Perkins."

"You did? But you talked soft, Andy?"

"I done as well as I could. He said that boys will be boys, and then, all at once, I wanted to take him by the throat. It came to me like a fit. I fought it off, and I was weak afterward."

"Did you say anything?"

"Not a word, but Jim Perkins went to the door with me, looking scared, and he said that he'd see that they was no more stones thrown at Sally." The very memory of his anger made Andy change, and his mouth grew straight and hard.

"Then Sally doesn't get on very well with the folks in town?" asked Hal Dozier. He himself had been too much on his big ranch of late to follow things in Martindale closely.

"She gets on with the kids pretty fine but, if a man comes near her, she tries to take a chunk out of him with her teeth, or brain him with her heels. There was young Canning the other day . . . he just jumped the fence in time."

He broke into riotous laughter.

"Wait a minute," cut in the marshal. "There seems to be two sides to this story. Is that a laughing matter? Canning might have been killed!"

"Served him right for teasing her."

The marshal shook his head.

"You'd better see Hulan," he suggested.

After a little more talk Andrew accepted the advice. The Hulan ranch was neighbor to the town. He would be practically in Martindale, and all that he wanted was to convince Martindale of his honest determination to reform. Saying good-bye to the marshal, he went straight to the hotel.

Chapter Six
Martindale Declares War

Business was slack, men were plentiful on the range at this season, so Andrew was not the only one who went to the hotel to call on old Si Hulan. He found that the rancher was in his room interviewing the applicants one by one. He had three vacancies, and he intended to fill them all, but only after he had seen every man who was asking for a place. There were a dozen men on the verandah, all waiting to be seen or, having been seen, they waited for the selection of the rancher. They were playing together like a lot of great, senseless puppies, working off practical jests that caused more pain than laughter, and every man was sharp eyed for a chance to take advantage of his fellow. Even as Andy approached, someone happened to turn his head as he walked down the verandah. Instantly he was tripped and sent pitching across the porch. He stopped his fall by thrusting both arms into the back of another who was driven catapulting down the steps. This man in turn attempted to stop his momentum by breaking the shock at the expense of Andy Lanning.

The latter had his back turned, but a running shadow warned him, and he leaped aside. The other rushed past with arms stretched out, grinning.

There was a sudden cessation of laughter on the porch as Andrew turned. The man, who had attempted to knock him down from behind, came to a stumbling halt and faced about, deadly pale, his lips twitching, and the expectancy of the men on the verandah was a thing to be felt like electricity in the air. It was very clear to Andy that they expected him to take offense and, being a gunman, to show his offense by drawing his revolver. The white, working face of the big fellow before him told the same story. The man was terribly afraid, facing death, and certain of his destruction. But his great brown hand was knotted about the butt of his gun, and he would not give way. Rather die, to be sure, than be shamed before so many. Pity came to Andy, and he smiled into the eyes of the other.

"They's no harm done, partner," he said gently and went up on the verandah.

He left the big man behind him, stunned. Presently the latter went to the hitching rack, got his horse, and rode down the street. He would tell his children and his grandchildren in later years how he faced terrible Andy Lanning and came away with his life.

The crowd on the verandah began to break out of their silence again, but the former mirth was not restored. A shadow of dread had passed over them, and their spirits were still dampened. Covertly every eye watched Andrew. He went gloomily up the steps and laid his hand on the back of the first chair he saw, just as another man came hurriedly from the interior of the hotel.

"Hey," he called, "my chair, you!"

Andrew turned, and the newcomer stopped, as though he had received a blow in the face.

"I made a mistake," he said.

"Take your chair," replied Andrew gravely. "There are plenty more."

The other moistened his white lips. "I don't want it," he said unevenly. "Besides, I'm going right back inside."

Before Andrew could speak again the latter had turned and gone hastily through the door. Lanning sat down, buried in gloom. Dead silence reigned along the verandah now. He knew what was in their thoughts—that twice they had come within the verge of seeing gun play.

And he writhed at the thought. Did they think he was a professional bully to take advantage of them? He knew, as well as they knew, that an ordinary man had no ghost of a chance against his trained speed of hand and steadiness of nerve and lightning accuracy of eye. Did they think he would force issues on them? Yet he felt bitterly that, sooner or later, they would actually herd him into a mortal fight. Indeed one of these boys would not wait to ask questions. If he crossed the path of Lanning by chance, he would take it for granted that guns were the order of the day and draw his weapon. And then what was the chance of Andy, except to kill, or be killed?

Decidedly the marshal was right. He must get onto the Hulan ranch and let Martindale grow more gradually acclimated to the changed Andrew Lanning. He knew that this position of his was one which many a bullying gunfighter had labored years to attain and had gloried in, but to him it was a horror. He wanted to stand up before them and tell them they were wrong. But he had tried that on the first day of his return to the town, and he had seen in every face the conviction that he lied.

He was glad when it came his turn to see Hulan and, as he stepped through the door into the inner hall, he heard the murmur of voices break out again on the verandah in subdued whispers, and he knew that they were talking of him.

Old Si Hulan greeted him with amazing warmth. He was a stringy old man who had once been bulkily strong and was still active. Age had diminished him, but it had not crippled him. His lean, much-wrinkled face lighted, and he came out from behind the table to grip the hand of Andrew.

"Why, son," he said, "are you hunting for work on my ranch?"

"That's it," said Andy. He had never known the old man well, and this generous greeting warmed his heart.

"You are? Then I'll tell a man that this is my lucky day. I been looking for your make of a man for a long time. Sit down, lad. Sit down and lemme look you over."

The Return of Free Range Lanning

He pushed Andrew into a chair. "In the old days they didn't think much of you. I've heard 'em talk, the idiots! But I knowed that a Lanning was always a Lanning, same as a hawk is always a hawk, even if a chicken does the hatching."

He kept grinning and chuckling to himself in the pauses of his talk.

"You go back and get your blankets," he said, "and get ready to come along with me this evening. Or, if you ain't got blankets, it don't make any difference. I'll fix you up like a king. I'll give you an outfit any rider on the range would be proud of."

"That's mighty fine," returned Andy, amazed by this cordiality. "About the wages you can fix your own price. I'm pretty green at ranch work."

"We'll agree on wages," said the old man. "Ain't any trouble on that head."

"Another thing you ought to know before you take me on. My hoss ain't very good at working cattle. Matter of fact I wouldn't even train her for that job. But if it's just riding the range, she'll be fine for that. But not for a lot of roping and heavy work."

It seemed that Si Hulan was daunted by these remarks.

"Roping?" he demanded. "Roping? You? Why, boy, d'you think I'm going to use a mountain lion to pull a wagon? Cow work! Ride the range!" He rocked back on his heels, tucked his thumbs into the armholes of his vest and burst into a roar of laughter.

"Son," he said, when he found his voice again, "you hark to me. The job I got for you is right in your own line." He lowered his tone, and his eyes twinkled discreetly. "Up yonder in the hills I got the finest little layout for moonshining that ever you see. I raise my own grain, you see, and I feed it into my own still. Nothing easier. And I got the still cached away where the best fox in the police service would never find it. Well, Andy, what I'm going to use you for is running that moonshine over the hills and down to the river. That's where I market it. I got a tough gang of boys working the run for me now, but what I need is a leader that'll keep 'em in order. And you're the man for me. I guess they ain't any of 'em so hard but what they'll soften up when Andy Lanning gives 'em an order. As for the wages they ain't going to be none. You and me will just split up the profit, almost any reasonable way you say. I furnish the goods, and you take what little risk they is. It ain't really no big risk. It's for running the men that I want you."

He had kept up his harangue so closely and with such a hot enthusiasm that Andrew could not interrupt him until he reached this point, and he interrupted by rising from the chair into which Si Hulan had thrust him.

"Mister Hulan," he said slowly, "you got me all wrong. I'm going straight. I'm staying inside the law as long as the law will let me. Run your own still. It's nothing to me, but I'll have no hand in it."

Hulan gasped. Then he nodded.

"I see," he said. "Trying me out? I don't blame you for being mistrustful of folks after what you've been doing the past few years, but. . . ."

"First and last and all the time," said Andrew, "I mean what I say. I'm going straight, Hulan. I can't take that job. But, if you got an honest job running cattle on the range, let me take a try at it, and I'll thank you for the chance. I don't care what the wages are."

Hulan snorted, a flush growing up his withered face.

"That's the song, is it?" he asked. "D'you think I'm a fool, Lanning? D'you think you have anybody in this town fooled? Don't you suppose everybody knows that you're in here on some crooked job?"

His voice became a growl.

"I'll tell you one thing that may surprise you. You wonder why nobody has asked you to step out of town, why we've been so simple we've let you stay and make your plans and your plots, whatever they may be. But we ain't been sleeping, Andy. Not by a long sight! They's five of the best men in this town has got together and sworn to keep a hoss saddled night and day, ready to jump on your trail and run you down the minute you make your break.

And we got other towns all posted, so we can get in touch with them *pronto*, the minute you tear loose.

"Why am I telling you all this? Simply to show you where you stand. No, Lanning, once wrong always wrong, and we know it. That's why I make you my offer. Come out with me and I'll cover up your tracks. If you stay down here and try to work your game, we'll get you the minute you step crooked. Why, you fool, we been holding our breath ever since you come in, waiting for a chance to nail you!"

Andrew Lanning watched him gloomily. It was all in line with the attitude of the younger men on the verandah of the hotel. It was perfectly plain now. They hated him; they feared him; and they would get him if they dared. They would bide their time. If appearances were against him for a moment, they would make their play. The governor of the state had pardoned him, but society had not forgiven him, would not forgive him. With a breaking heart he saw the vision of Anne Withero, the happiness of which he had dreamed, grow dim and flicker out into complete darkness.

He turned slowly away from Hulan and stepped into the hall and then slowly down the stairs. As he went, anger rose in him and swelled his heart. It was unfair, cruelly unfair. In some way they should be made to pay for their stupidity. He hated them all!

At the bottom of the stairs he came upon a knotted little group, standing with their heads together, listening to some jest or gossip.

"Get out of the way!" said Andy Lanning angrily.

They jerked their heads aside, saw him, and then melted back from his path. Andrew strode through them without deigning a glance in either direction. He detested them as much as they feared him. If they wanted war, let it be war. He heard the whisper stir behind him, but he strode on through the door and went slowly down the steps to the ground. War, indeed, had been declared.

Chapter Seven
The Call of His Kind

Through the little town of Martindale a single whisper traveled as distinctly and as swiftly as the report of a cannon down a small gorge. Hal Dozier heard of the first outbreak of the ex-outlaw ten minutes after it happened. He went straight to the hotel and found a grave conclave deliberating on the verandah. There was no sign of the usual jesting, or the usual tales. They crowded their heads close together and talked with frowns. The marshal knew that serious trouble was in the air.

He was more alarmed than ever when they fell silent at his approach. He singled out Si Hulan, who was among the rest, and put the question to him.

"What's wrong with Andy Lanning?"

"What's wrong? Everything's wrong with him. He's no good," said the old rancher with deliberation. "I offer him a job with me, a regular, honest job at good pay," continued Hulan, lying smoothly, "and the infernal young hound asked me what he got on the side. I asked him what he meant by that. He said I ought to know that he wasn't interested in small-fry talk. He wanted action and big pay, and he didn't care for the danger. That's the sort of talk he gave me. I told him to get out of my room and never let me see his face again. And he went, growling!"

Hal Dozier scented the lie under this talk. He had known Hulan for a long time as a man of dubious life, but now it was impossible for him directly to challenge the statement. All he could say was: "It doesn't sound like Andy. He doesn't talk that way, Hulan."

"Not to you. Sure he don't talk that way to you," said

The Return of Free Range Lanning

Hulan. "He's pulled the wool over your eyes and made a fool of you, Hal. Everybody in town knows it except you, and it's time that you be told. That kid comes to you and makes good talk, says he's going to reform. The rest of us know that he's gone wrong. Once wrong always wrong. He's going to the bad, and you're a fool to let him take you in."

A younger man could not have talked quite so frankly to the formidable marshal. But Si Hulan was too old to be in danger of physical attack, and he spoke his mind outright to Dozier.

He went on: "You've made a pet out of this mankiller, Hal. That's bad enough for you, because one of these days he'll turn and sink his teeth in you. But it's particular bad for us in this here town, because you ain't the only one he's apt to muss up. I say it wasn't square to bring him in."

There was a gloomy murmur from the others, and Hal Dozier studied them in despair. One by one they told the story of how Lanning had come down the stairs and ordered the crowd to separate so that he could walk through. They told the tale profanely and expressively, and they assured the marshal that, the next time such a thing happened they would not stand upon the order of procedure, they would fall upon young Andrew Lanning and teach him manners.

"Boys," said the marshal gravely, "I know how you feel. You think that Lanning is taking advantage of you because he's a proved gunfighter. Maybe it looks that way but, if I could get close to this trouble, I know I could show you that you'd badgered Andy into it. He ain't a bully. He never was, and he never will be. But they's some around this town that's been treating him like he was a bear to be baited. Well, boys, if you ever tease Andy to the point when he breaks loose, he'll turn out the worst rampaging bear you ever see. Keep that under your hat, but give Andy a chance to make good, which he can do!"

With this mixture of cajoling and warning, Hal left the hotel and sought Lanning. He found his young protégé buried in gloom in the silent blacksmith shop. Andrew lifted his head slowly and greeted his friend with a lack-luster eye.

"Keep your heart up," advised the marshal. "Work will begin to come in to you, son. This old shop will be full of business all day long, as soon as the boys in town are sure you mean to settle down. You were a good black-smith in the old days, and they know it. But no more busting out like you done today."

It was proof of the despair of Andrew that even to Hal Dozier he did not offer the true explanation of that affair. He let it go.

"Hal," he said sadly, "the main trouble is that I don't think I want the work to come in. I was a blacksmith in the old days. I liked it, and I liked to make things. But it doesn't interest me any more."

"What in the world are you, then?"

"I dunno, Hal. I can't find out. Maybe I'm what they figure me to be, no good!"

The marshal found that he had no answer ready, and he could only make one suggestion.

"If you can't make a go of the blacksmith work, come with me. I'll make you a deputy. They's a big bunch of cash right now over in the bank, and they have been ask-ing me for a good man to guard it. Will you let me give them your name?"

But Andy shook his head. "They wouldn't take me. Be-sides, I'm not ready to give up yet."

Hal Dozier went straight to the telegraph office and wired to Anne Withero: "Come quick, or not at all."

In the evening he received an answer from Anne With-ero, saying she was coming on the next train. That tele-gram gave him heart. But would Andrew Lanning hold out until the arrival of this great ally?

The marshal did not know it, but the great temptation was coming to Andrew even at that very moment. He sat in the old shack which his uncle, Jasper Lanning, had owned before him. Never had it seemed more dreary, more deserted. Coming home from the shop at the end of the idle day, little Judy had crossed the street to avoid passing close to him, and that told Andy more than the curses of a crowd of grown men what the town thought of him.

He felt the blight of it cold in his heart all the time that he was cooking his supper, and then he sat down to the meal without appetite. The bacon was cold, the flapjacks soggy, the potatoes half cooked. He forced himself to eat.

All the windows were open, for the night was coming on close and windless, and he wished to take advantage of every stir of the air. It was very hot, and it seemed to have grown hotter since the coming of the darkness. The little flame of the lantern seemed to add to it. He could feel the glow against his face, and there was the nauseating odor of kerosene and the foul-burning wick. But he had not heart enough to trim the wick and freshen the light.

When he had finished his meal, there was the doubly disagreeable duty of washing the dishes. The water was greasy to the touch, nauseating again. The walls of the kitchen were hung with shadows, memories of the old days, and those old days seemed cramped and disagreeable. He was returning to that life and there was no glamour to it. It was like crawling into a hole and waiting for death.

He finished his task by banging the dishpan onto its nail on the rough-finished boards of the wall and strode slowly back to the other room. There he sat down with a book, but the print would not take hold of his eye. He found the book falling to his lap, while his mind wandered through the past. He had lived greater things than were in these romantic pages. He had been part and parcel and the prime mover in deeds that had stirred the length and the breadth of the mountain desert. And a faint, grim smile played and grew and died on his lips, as he remembered some of them.

He was recalled from his dreaming sharply, as though by a voice. All at once, though he did not change from his position, he was tinglingly alert. Another person had entered the room and stood at the door behind him. An added sense, which only men who have been hunted possess, informed him of that fact. Someone was there. His mind flashed over a score of possibilities of men who hated him, men who might have trailed him to the town to wreak vengeance. Any one of them would be capable of shooting him in the back without warning.

All this went through his mind in the least part of a second. Then in a flash he whirled out of his chair, slipping into the dense shadow on the floor with the speed of a snake that twists and strikes. As he fell the long gun, which never left his hip, was gleaming in his hand.

The man at the door jerked both empty hands above his head and cursed softly. He was a handsome fellow with a rather colorless face, bright eyes, and an alert, straight carriage.

"Don't shoot!" he called. "Don't shoot, Andy!"

The latter came softly to his feet, but still crouched, panting and savage under the urge of that swift impulse to fight. He kept low in the shadow which washed across the room, below the level of the table on which the squat lantern sat. In this shadow Andy slipped to the farther corner of the room. There he was in a position which neither the two windows nor the open door commanded. Here he straightened, still with the revolver ready.

"You can drop your hands now, Scottie," he ordered.

Scottie had turned slowly to follow the movements of Lanning, always with his arms stiffly above his head.

"Whispering winds," he exclaimed, as he brought his hands down. "Fast as ever, eh? Thought you'd be slowed up a little by the quiet life, but you're not."

"What's up?" demanded Andrew Lanning. "And what d'you want, Scottie? Is there anyone outside?"

"Nobody that means you any harm. Suspicious, aren't you, these days? How does that come, Andy? Living among these fine, quiet, honest men in Martindale I should think that your life would be like a smooth-flowing river."

He grinned impishly at Lanning.

The Return of Free Range Lanning

"You've said enough," said Andy. It was a new man who faced Scottie, a dangerous, cunning, agile man whose eyes never ceased roving from door to window to the face of his guest. "Why are you here?"

Scottie sauntered to a chair and dropped into it, his hands folded behind his head. In this fashion, with a slow and lordly turning of the eyes, he surveyed the house.

"Not a lot to boast of as a house, Andy. Why am I here? Why, just for a chat. Dropped in to chat about old days, you know, Andy. The way you sat there, with your book upside down and your eye looking at nothing, I thought you might be thinking of the same thing. What about it?"

Andy watched him carefully, but he dropped the gun back in the holster.

"Well, Scottie?"

The latter refused to be pinned down to reasons and purposes. He rambled on.

"Any of our camps could beat this, eh? In the old days when Allister led us around? Those were free times, Andy. Money, liquor, good cigars, best chuck on the range. Can you come over that here in Martindale?"

Andy was silent. Into his mind had flashed a picture of the camp fire and the circle of faces bathed in yellow light and carved from black shadow.

"But I suppose you got friends down here who more than make up for what you miss, eh?"

There was a flash and twinkle in his bright eyes. How unlike the eyes of any man Lanning had seen in Martindale since his return. For the wolf light was in them and, as his heart leaped in response, he knew that the wolf light was in his own eyes. He knew that if he lived a long and peaceful life to the very end, that light would gleam from time to time in his face, and the fierce, free, joyous urge would pulse and rush through his veins. It was in him, and it was part of him. When he spoke to Scottie, like spoke to like. One word between them might mean more than a whole conversation with the men of Martindale. Two glances were question and reply.

"Leave out my Martindale friends," said Andy dryly.

Max Brand

"Why are you here? And who came with you?"

"I came alone."

Andy smiled.

"You're right, chief," said Scottie. "You know I wouldn't risk coming down here alone."

"Who's with you?"

"Ask."

Andy whistled a prolonged, low note that traveled far and quavered up at the end weirdly. After a moment there came a still softer answer.

"Larry la Roche and Clune, eh? Where's the big fellow?"

Scottie made a careless gesture of lighting a match and blowing it out.

"Dead?" asked Andy huskily.

"Dead."

"How?"

"They cornered him at Old Willow, Jordan and his two cubs of kids. Jordan came up and talked to him. His kids sneaked around behind and drilled him."

Andy began to pace up and down lightly, swiftly, soundlessly.

"I wish I'd been there!" he said. "Jordan, eh?"

"I wish you'd been there," replied Scottie. "The big fellow would never have dropped out if you'd been there to lead. But the rest of us couldn't handle him, and now he's done for. As a matter of fact, chief, the three of us have come down here to make a little proposition to you."

He leaned forward, his elbows sprawling out on the table.

"Lanning, will you listen?"

Andrew hesitated and, before he could answer, Scottie struck smoothly into his talk.

"Chief, we need you back. I admit that we did a dirty trick. I admit that you've reason not to trust us. Particularly me. But you were getting Hal Dozier off free, and every one of us hates Hal Dozier like poison, and has reason to! We couldn't stand it. I couldn't stand it. I made a mistake and tried to get Dozier, whether you wanted to or not. Well, I didn't do it. You turned out faster in the head and stronger than the whole lot of us. I admit it, Andy. I'm older than you are. I've followed the game a lot longer than you've followed it, but I'll freely admit that, next to Allister, you're the best leader that ever rode the mountains. And time will give you as much or more than Allister had.

"Clune and Larry la Roche and I are three good men. You know that. But, without a leader, we play lone hands, and we get poor results. And what leader can we get? I tried to hold the boys together. I couldn't do it. I'm ashamed to admit it, but it's true. Then we agreed to follow Larry, but he's too hot headed, just as you told us a long time ago. Matter of fact we thought you were too young to know much. It's taken the last few months to teach us that you knew a lot more than we gave you credit for. In short, we agree that we have to have you back.

"Allister picked you to follow him in the lead, and Allister was right. You were next best man to him. We see that now. If you come to us, you'll be the chief, just as Allister was, and you'll settle the disputes, decide on the plans, and take two shares for yourself every time we split the pot. How does that sound to you, Andy?"

Lanning opened his lips to speak and then sank into a chair, with something like a groan.

"No!" he declared.

"Lad, we need you!"

"Clear out, Scottie," said Andrew.

"But I'm coming back," said Scottie, rising, but smiling in the face of Andrew. "I'm coming back and, when I come back, I'll get another answer. Remember, Andy, we're three who can do more than three things, and with you to organize and keep us together we'll live like kings, free kings, Andy! You're not cut out for life in a dump like this. Don't forget, I'm coming back."

"Don't do it," replied Andrew. "I've given you my answer. Stay away!"

But Scottie laughed mockingly, waved from the doorway, and disappeared into the deep, hot black of the night.

Andrew stared after him with trembling lips, and his deep agitation showed in his face. He had to fight hard to keep from following.

Chapter Eight
Iron Dust

There had been strange men in Martindale, but none stranger than the man who arrived the next morning. It would have been hard to imagine one less in tune and in touch with his surroundings. The slouching, loose-dressed, careless cowpunchers on the hotel verandah stared at him askance, as he came up the steps. He wore a little low-crowned, narrow-brimmed derby, a low collar, very tight for the bull-like neck, close-fitting clothes, through which the rolling muscles of his shoulders bulged under the coat, rubber-heeled shoes, square and comfortably blunt of toe.

When he signed his name on the register, he seemed to be trying to dig the pen through the paper, and the name sprawled huge and legible at a great distance: "J. J. Gruger." While he waited to be taken to his room, he snapped a tailor-made cigarette out of a box and lighted it with singular dexterity.

He was the sort of man the cowboys would ordinarily have laughed at, almost openly. But there was something muscularly intense about the bulldog face of J. J. Gruger that discouraged laughter, and his eyes had a way of jerking from place to place and lingering a piercing instant, wherever they fell.

He was only a moment in his room upstairs and then he came down. With short, springy steps he proceeded to the dining room and ate hugely. After that he came out onto the verandah, not to lounge about, but as one on business bent. He did not approve of Martindale any more than Martindale approved of him, and he was not

Max Brand

at all eager to disguise his emotions. Having surveyed the whitehot, dusty street he turned with a characteristic suddenness upon one of the loungers who was no less a person than Si Hulan.

But the address of Lefty Gruger was not nearly so jerky and blunt as one would have expected from his demeanor. He drew up a chair beside Si, who eyed him curiously, and leaned a little toward the crafty old rancher. In his manner there was a sort of confiding interest, as though he were imparting a secret of great value. And he talked rather from the side of his mouth, gauging his voice so accurately that the sound traveled as far as the ear of Si Hulan and not an inch farther.

"Name's Gruger," he said by way of introduction. "I'm up here looking for a bird called Lanning. Got any dope on him, or is he a stranger to you?"

"More or less," said Si. "He's twenty-five or twenty-six years old, and I've knowed him along about twenty-four years, I reckon. But I wouldn't say we was ever familiar-like."

There was a little glint in the quick eyes of Lefty as they traveled over the face of his companion. In some subtle way the two came to an understanding on the spot.

"If you mean you ain't a friend of this guy," said Lefty, "it don't bother me none. I ain't his brother myself. But can you tell me anything about him?"

Si Hulan cleared his throat and paused, as if making up his mind how far he could go. Then he felt his way as he spoke.

"Lanning was a nice, quiet kid around town," he said. "Nobody had nothing ag'in him, thought he was kind of spineless, as a matter of fact. All at once he busted loose. Got to be a regular fighter, a gunfighter!"

He waited to see if this shot had taken effect.

"You don't say," said Lefty with polite interest.

"Maybe you don't know what a gunfighter is, friend," observed Hulan.

"Maybe not," said Lefty guilelessly.

"It means a gent who lives with his gun day and night

and never lets it get more than an inch or so out of his hand. He practices all the time. Tries the draw, tries himself at a mark, and gets ready to use that gun in a fight to kill. And the usual windup is that he gets so blamed skillful that he ends by trying himself out and picking fights till he drops somebody. Then he's outlawed and goes to the devil."

"But I sort of get it that young Lanning ain't gone to the devil yet."

"Son," said Si Hulan, who now seemed to feel at ease with the stranger, "that boy is rapping at Satan's door, and he'll get inside pretty *pronto*."

"Uh . . . huh," said Lefty Gruger.

"Yesterday he made a little bust," said Si Hulan. "He's been here with us a few days, trying to make out that he figures on living real quiet. But yesterday he sort of busted loose. And now we're sitting around waiting for him to make a play. And the minute he pulls a gun, he'll be salted down. He's no good. Once wrong always wrong."

"You've said a mouthful, pal," observed Lefty Gruger.

His little eyes twinkled with thought for a moment. Then he sat up and hailed a freckle-faced youngster passing the verandah.

"Son," he said, "will you go find Andrew Lanning for me and tell him there's a man waiting for him at the hotel."

He followed the request with the bright arc of a quarter that spun into the clutching hand of the boy. The latter stared at the generous stranger for a moment, then dug his bare toes inches deep in the dust and gave himself a flying start down the street. Lefty Gruger watched him thoughtfully. An idea had come to him which he considered, for its simplicity and its effectiveness, to be the equal of any he had ever had in his entire criminal career. A glow of satisfaction with himself spread through him. It was a conclusive proof that the enforced idleness of his career in the prison had not dulled his wits a particle.

Presently he eluded a question of Si Hulan, slipped out

of his chair, and began to walk up and down in front of the verandah, gradually increasing his distance until he was out of earshot of the men on the verandah—out of earshot as long as only a conversational tone was used. This was the strategic point which he wished to attain and, when the voices on the verandah had faded to a blur behind him, he halted, settled his hat more firmly to shade his eyes, and waited, cursing the dazzling flare of the sunlight from the dust of the street.

He had hardly reached this position when he saw his quarry coming. He knew the man as well as if a herald had gone before, announcing that this was Andrew Lanning. The bold, free step, the well-poised head, and something, moreover, of hair-trigger alertness about the man convinced him that this was the gunfighter, this was certainly the man of action.

Lefty slipped his hand into his coat pocket and ran the tips of his fingers lovingly over the familiar outlines of the automatic. He withdrew his hand, bringing out a cigarette box, and took out and lighted his smoke with his usual speed. He had snapped the match away, and it was fuming in the dust when Andrew Lanning came close.

Lefty surveyed him with a practiced eye. The promise from the distance was more than borne out in the details which he observed at close hand. Here was a man among many men. Here was a foeman worthy, almost, of his own steel. A sort of honest enthusiasm welled up in the heart of Lefty Gruger, just as the boxer feels a savage joy when his own first blow of the battle is deftly blocked and a jarring return thuds home against head and breast. Lefty Gruger measured his enemy and felt that the battle might well be close.

"You're Lanning," he said smilingly, and held out his stubby hand.

It was very essential that he should be seen by the verandah crowd to greet Andrew Lanning amiably. He could not resist the temptation, however, and allowed some of his bull strength to go into the grip. There was an amazing reaction. His own bulky hand had hardly be-

The Return of Free Range Lanning

gun to tighten before the lithe, long fingers of Andrew curled up and became so many bands of contracting steel, cutting into flesh and grinding sinews against bone. It was only a moment. Then their hands fell apart, and Lefty Gruger felt the life slowly return to his numbed muscles.

He maintained his smile for the benefit of those on the verandah. Then he shifted his position as to bring Andrew facing the verandah, while he kept his own back turned.

"I'm Gruger," he said, continuing the introduction. "I've dropped out here on a little piece of business with you. A sort of private business, Lanning. I didn't know how to tackle it, but I got a couple of hints from the birds on the verandah. They sure love you a lot in this burg, Lanning."

"They seem to," said Andy coldly. "What did they tell you about me?"

"Not much, but enough. Tipped me that you were a gunfighter and a fire-eater and that they were just sitting around waiting for you to bust loose, which played right into my hand. Gives me a chance to do what I want to do, right in public. It's about the first time that I've ever had an audience. And say, bo, I sure love applause!"

"I don't understand," said Andrew, falling back a pace, the better to study the half-grinning, half-ugly face of Gruger.

"Why, Kid," continued Lefty, "I've come out here to bump you off, and I find that I can do the job and get a vote of thanks and my traveling expenses out of the town. That's easy, ain't it?"

Andrew blinked. It seemed that the chunky stranger must be either mad or jesting.

"I'm talking straight," said Lefty, dropping his voice to an ominous purr. "Kid, go for your gat. I've showed the folks that I've met you peaceable and all that. Now you got to go for your gat, and I'll do my best to drop you."

"I understand," said Andrew huskily. "They worked up the job, eh? Found a mankiller to fit my case and now

Max Brand

. . . but it won't work, Gruger. I've made up my mind to see this thing through. I'm going to live without gun fights. One gunfight is ruin for me. One more gunfight makes me what you are."

"You lie!" said Lefty, letting his voice ring out suddenly. "I tell you, you lie!" He added in a murmur: "Now get the gun, you fool! Get the gun, or I'll shame you so you won't be able to show your face around this town again as long as you live."

The voices on the verandah had ceased. Men had scattered to shelter. From shelter they watched and listened. If someone had offered five dollars for the life of the stranger, the offer would have been received with ardent laughter. But still there was no gun play, even after Andy Lanning had been given the lie. They could see, also, that his face was white.

"It doesn't work," he was saying huskily. "Gruger, I won't fight."

"Take this then!" said Lefty, and his sturdy arm flicked out. The clap of his open hand against the face of Lanning was plainly audible to the listeners and the watchers, and their muscles tightened against the coming report of the guns.

But a miracle happened. While Lefty shot his hand back into his pocket and twitched up the muzzle of his automatic, prepared to send out that spurt of fire and lead with the touch of his forefinger, the hand of Andy Lanning had darted down to the butt of his gun and stayed there. He maintained the struggle for an instant, fighting bitterly against himself, and then he conquered. He turned on his heel and strode back down the street, his cheek tingling where the fingers of Lefty had struck him.

Lefty went back to the hotel as one stunned. He was greeted with a clamor of frank awe and applause.

"By heaven," said Si Hulan, "they all got a yaller streak, all these gunfighters, and it took this nervy little bulldog

206

to bring it out. Son, come up to my room. I got a bottle to set out for you *pronto*, best in the land."

Lefty Gruger accompanied him thoughtfully, saying not a word

Chapter Nine
Annie Laurie

Dazed, sick with longing to turn back and find the man again, Andy Lanning fought his way home. All the wolf that Scottie had wakened in him the night before came back to him with redoubled force.

He hurried to the shop, and there he frantically smashed a big bar of iron into useless shapes with the blows of a twelve-pound sledge. All his rage went into that labor. When it was ended, he was weak, but his spirit was quieter, and he dragged himself slowly toward his home. He passed the open door of the rival smith's shop and saw his competitor leaning there, filling a pipe at the end of a prosperous day. At sight of Andy he nodded carelessly, and Andy suspected that the sudden frown with which the big, sooty fellow looked down at his fuming pipe was for the purpose of veiling a smile.

No doubt he had heard of the disgrace of Andrew Lanning earlier in the day. Now that he had once been braved, others would probably try it. How long could he endure? How long?

He was trembling with the mental struggle when he reached his shack and flung himself down on his bunk, his head in his hands. How long he remained there he could not tell, fighting always against that terrific impulse to rise and hunt out his persecutor. But, when a hand touched his shoulder, he lifted himself to a sitting posture. It was so dark that he could barely make out the face of Scottie.

"I've heard," said Scottie, "and I've understood. But is it worth the gaff, Andy?"

The Return of Free Range Lanning

The words fell like a blessing on Lanning. Scottie was more or less of a gentleman in training, more or less educated. His trained mind had understood. But how many more would?

"The rest of 'em," said Scottie, "are saying that you've showed yellow . . . the fools!"

"La Roche and Clune are saying that?" asked Andrew, rising.

"They? Of course not! They saw you go down to face Hal Dozier. I mean the rest of the town. They're laughing at you, Andy, and you're a butt and a joke among 'em. Now, partner, the time has come. Sally is ready and waiting outside. Come on with me, Andy. The best of it is that our first job, after you come to us is in this town, this night! They'll curse themselves before the morning comes for having turned down Andrew Lanning."

Andy went hastily to the door. Sally, from the shed, saw the outline of his form and neighed very softly.

"Ah, Sally girl," exclaimed poor Andy, "are you asking me to go, too?"

"Because you'd be a fool not to go. It's fate, Andy. You can't get away from that."

A child's voice began singing down the street, a shrill, sweet, eager voice, breaking and trembling on the high notes. Little Judy was coming, singing "Annie Laurie" with all her heart.

"Hush!" said Andy, and raised his hand.

The outlaw remained silent, frowning in the gloom of the twilight. He knew that that child's song was fighting against him and saving Andy from temptation. The voice passed and died away down the street.

"No," declared Andy at last. "I thank you for trusting me and asking me to lead you, Scottie, but I can't go."

"If it's for that girl," broke out Scottie, "I can tell you that she'll never think of. . . ."

"That'll hold you now," said Andy warningly. "Leave her out of it."

"Lanning," began Scottie again, "if I go back without you the boys will call me. . . ."

"A fool," said Andy, "and maybe you are. Besides, you're a good deal of a snake, Scottie. I trusted you once, and you tried to get me. You'll have no second chance. No matter how I throw in, if I leave Martindale with every man's hand against me, I won't throw in with you and the rest of 'em. You played me dirt once, and I know well you would do it again in a pinch. Now get out!"

Scottie, after hesitating through one moment of savage silence, turned and went.

Left to the darkness, Andy sank down on his bunk, his head between his hands. He had cut loose, it seemed, from every anchor. He had severed connections with the very outlaws who might have been his port of last refuge. Having already alienated the men of Martindale, he had also sacrificed the one thing which should have remained to him when all else was gone, his pride.

Chapter Ten
Four of a Kind

Scottie went hastily through the dark and, rounding the corner of Sally's shed, found two figures drawn back so as to melt into the shadow under the projecting roof.

"Well?"

"Missed, curse him!" said Scottie.

A soft volley of invectives answered him.

"I knew you would," said the hard, nasal voice of La Roche. "Stubborn as rock once he's made up his mind."

"You know a pile after a thing's done," declared Clune.

"Shut up," commanded Scottie. "The thing's settled. No fighting about it."

"But what'll we do for the fourth man? That's a four-man job we got on hand," declared Larry la Roche. "The fourth man, that's the first thing we got to get."

"The first thing is to get back at Lanning," said Scottie venomously. "He called us a lot of treacherous snakes. He cursed you, Larry la Roche. He said he might come back and lead us if it weren't for your ugly face. He says he hates the thought of you. I told him, if he didn't want you, we didn't want him."

"Did he say that?" demanded La Roche, his tall body swaying back and forth in an ecstasy of repressed rage.

"And he said Clune was a cowardly fox, not worth having."

"I'll cut his throat to stop his gabble," declared Clune. "How come you to stand for such talk?"

"Because I'm not a gunfighter," said Scottie, writhing as he remembered the remarks which Andy had leveled at him in person. "But let's forget Andy for a while and think about the job. We'll get Lanning later on."

"Do we have to have four men?"

"One to watch in front, one behind, two inside. Yep, we have to have four. Who'll the fourth man be?"

"It just pops into my head," said Scottie thoughtfully, "that the fellow who bluffed out Lanning today might be our man."

"Did you see him?"

"Just from a distance. I'm not advertising my face around town. But he looks like a tough mug. He's at the hotel. Suppose we nab him."

"In the hotel?"

"No, you fool. Am I going to walk through the hotel and take a chance on being recognized?"

"Then where'll we find him?"

"If he tried to get Lanning once, he'll try again. Maybe he's simply been waiting for the dark. I'll wait down the street and stop him on the way. You stay here."

They obeyed, and Scottie turned the corner of the shed and sauntered around to the front of the shack, taking his position leaning against a hitching post, a little distance down the street from the hotel.

His reasoning about Lefty had been simple enough and, being simple, it was also justified. He had not been waiting in the place for twenty minutes when he saw a burly little figure come swaying through the twilight with short, choppy steps. Scottie stopped him with a soft hiss as he passed.

"One minute, partner."

"Eh?"

"Gruger," he said, "my name's Scottie. I know where you're going, and I'm here to stop you."

"Oh," murmured Lefty Gruger. "You think you'll stop me?"

"Because I hate to see a good man wasted. Gruger, he'll kill you if you force him to make a gun play."

"Say," asked Lefty, stepping close, "who are you, and what makes you think I'm going to force a gun play on anybody? Where do you come in?"

The Return of Free Range Lanning

"By needing you for another job that'll pay more."

"H-m," said Lefty Gruger, peering through the shadows, apparently more or less satisfied by what he saw.

"I'll undertake," said Scottie, "to prove that Lanning is a better man than you are with a gun. And then I'll prove that my job is worth more than the Lanning job."

"And suppose all this chatter meant something, suppose I was really after Lanning, how would doing your job help me to get rid of Lanning?"

"I have an idea," said Scottie smoothly, "of a way we can ruin Lanning with my job."

"Pal," said Lefty, after an instant of thought, "I like the sound of your talk. Start in by showing me how good Lanning is with a gat."

"Follow me," said Scottie.

He led the redoubtable Lefty Gruger around behind the shed and presently introduced him with a wave of the hand to Clune and Larry la Roche. Scottie then asked Lefty to accompany the trio over the hill and into the valley beyond. Lefty followed willingly enough, for there was sufficient mystery about this proceeding to attract him. They halted a full mile away in a broad, moonlit ravine, paved with pale-gray stone which gave the valley the brightness of twilight.

"Now," said Scottie to Larry la Roche, "I want you to get out your gun, Larry, and do a little shooting for us. You're the best of us with a gun."

"Thanks," replied Larry la Roche, "but I guess that don't make Clune none too happy. But what's there to shoot at? I'm willing."

"I'll give him a mark," suggested Lefty Gruger. He bent, picked up a piece of quartz, and shied it carelessly into the air. "Hit that!"

As he spoke the gun came into the hand of Larry, and the glitter of the falling quartz went out as though it had fallen out of the moonshine into shadow. Lefty Gruger remained staring where the quartz had last been seen, flashing dimly down through the air.

This was marksmanship indeed! But Lefty was not yet

convinced. As a snap shot he was a rare man himself.

"Turn your back," he said to Larry huskily, almost angrily.

Larry shoved the weapon back in the holster and obediently turned his back.

Lefty picked up a smaller rock and threw it high in the air. Not until it had reached the crest of its rise and was beginning its glinting descent did he call: "Now nail her!"

Larry la Roche whirled, the gun conjured mysteriously into his hand before his long body was halfway writhed around. His eye wandered and the muzzle of his gun wandered also, as he searched for the target. Then he fired. The rock glanced down again and was dropping into the shadow of a boulder when Larry fired the second time, and the little rock puffed into dust, white and glittering with crystals in the moonlight.

"All right," said Larry. "That was a hard one. What next?"

"What next?" asked Lefty Gruger. He passed his finger beneath his stiff collar, as if to make his breathing easier. "There ain't any more."

He continued to stare at Larry la Roche for a moment and then suddenly approached and held out his hand. He wrung the long fingers of Larry.

"Pal," he said, "I've seen shooting, and I've done some, but you got me beat."

It was the hardest speech that Lefty Gruger had ever compelled himself to make, but there was a basic honesty in the bottom of the soul of the killer, and it rang in his voice. He made a secret reservation, however, that shooting at a falling rock was far different from shooting at a human target. The latter might strike back at unknown speed. But it was not only the exquisite nicety of the marksmanship that stirred him. It was the careless grace with which the heavy gun had slipped into the bony fingers of the tall man, it was that lightning speed of mind which, having missed his elusive target once, enabled him to readjust to a new direction and fire again in the split part of a second later. The bullets had followed one

The Return of Free Range Lanning

second almost as swiftly as though they had spat from the muzzle of his automatic, and each had been a placed shot. No wonder that Lefty Gruger stepped back with a chilly feeling of awe descending upon him.

"Boys," he said, continuing that frankness which only a truly formidable man can show, "I didn't know they grew like you out in this part of the woods. I'm glad I bumped into you. But what's this got to do with me and young Lanning? How does this prove that he's a better man than I am?"

Scottie rubbed his chin, then he turned to Larry la Roche.

"Larry, you tell him."

Larry thought a moment, taking off his hat and turning it slowly in his hands, while his eyes wandered slowly along the back, sharp-cut line where the hills met the mysterious haze of the sky.

"I'll tell you," he said at length. "I been born and raised with a gun, and I took to it nacheral. It was a long time before I met a gent that was better'n me. But I met one. Yes, sir, he was sure a dandy with a gat. He could make a big gun talk to him like a pet. I can handle a gun pretty fair, but he didn't handle his gun. It was just a part of him. It growed into his hand, it growed into his mind. He just thought, and there was a dead man. Seemed like it, anyways. He was so fast with a gun and so straight that he didn't hardly ever shoot to kill. But he'd plug a gent in the arm or the leg and leave him behind."

Larry sighed.

"Say," said Lefty Gruger, tremendously impressed, "I'd have give ten years out of my life to seen him. I guess there never was a better'n him, eh?"

"There was," said Larry la Roche calmly. "Yep, there was a better than Allister. We never thought his equal would come along, but he came, and the man that beat him and killed him was Hal Dozier. He wasn't so fancy as Allister. He wasn't so smooth. Allister was fast as a cat's paw, but Hal Dozier is like the strike of a snake. He just explodes powder all the time, and when he fights they's a spark added, and he blows up. Well, he was faster than Allister and straighter with his gun, and he beat him fair and square."

"Boys," said Lefty Gruger, laughing uneasily, "I figure this ain't any country for me. This Hal Dozier is the champion of champions, eh? I'd hate to have him soft footing after me!"

"He ain't the champion," said Larry la Roche, "not by a long sight he ain't. They's a gent that beat Hal bad. Met him clean, man to man, and dropped him, shooting in moonlight dimmer'n this. A snake strikes plumb fast, but the end of a whip when it cracks is a pile faster. And that's the way with this other gent. He beat Hal Dozier."

"And who's he?"

"Andy Lanning."

Lefty Gruger took off his hat. He had become suffocatingly hot, and the perspiration was stinging his eyes.

"You get me now," murmured Scottie. "You see why I called you off him? Pal, you'll quit Lanning's trail?"

"I can't," said Lefty doggedly. "I give my word, and I stick to my word. I drop Lanning, or he drops me."

"But suppose," suggested Scottie softly, "that I show you how you make a barrel of loose coin and tie up Lanning at the same time. How would that suit you?"

"We'll talk about it, pal." He reverted to the last fascinating subject. "But this Lanning, how could he be so fast?"

"Listen," said Scottie, "and I'll tip you off. Allister and Hal Dozier are brave, you see? At least, Allister was, and Dozier is. They're afraid of nothing. They're plumb confident every time they fight. So's Larry la Roche, there. So's almost every gent who has a record as a gunman. But Lanning is different. He isn't hard as steel. He's all of a tremble when it comes to fight. I've seen him turn white as a girl and shake like a leaf before he went into danger. And he's always sure the other fellow will get him. He thinks it all out. He feels that he's as slow as a wagon wheel turning. He feels the other fellow's slug tearing through his body. He goes through agony before he fights but, when the time comes for the pull of the gun, he's a bundle of nerves, and every nerve is like loaded electricity. Well, partner, there's one thing faster than anything else, and that's the jump of an electric spark. That's what Lanning is when he fights."

"But he's a coward?"

"Don't fool yourself. He's just enough of a coward to get a thrill out of every time he pulls a gun. What booze is to some and cards to others and money to the rest, that's what gunfighting is to Lanning. It's the lion and he's the trainer. It's fear that brings the trainer into the cage every day, and it's fear that brings Lanning into trouble."

"But me and him. . . ."

"He says he's trying to go straight, curse him! He wouldn't fight because of that. Because, no matter how the trouble started, he knew that he'd be blamed for it. But you've crossed him, Lefty, and sooner or later, you lay to this, he'll get you and fill you full of lead unless you get him first. And the rest of us, the three of us, we all crossed him, too. We made this play tonight to try to get him back on our side. He wouldn't come. So we know he's going to try to get us, and our scheme is just to get him first."

"How?"

"By standing all together and using the law. Sit down, and I'll tell you how."

While he talked the moon slid high and higher and slipped into a cloud, and still the chief of the gang was outlining his plan. But, whatever that plan was, it did not develop that night. Martindale did not waken the next morning with the shudder which Scottie had planned for it the day before. It wakened calm and tired with the heat of the night and drifted into another blazing-hot day as peacefully as ever.

The night had been terrible for Andrew Lanning, and the day was more awful still, for he came to it physically exhausted, ragged nerves on edge. Sally came and put her head in at the window, as he washed his breakfast things, and afterward she glided at his side, as he went to the shop. But aside from Sally, there seemed no cheering note in all the universe, and the dark sense of defeat gathered more and more thickly in the corners of his brain.

That day dragged out, and another, with every waking hour filled with the suspicion of the men of Martindale and by Andrew's fear of himself. He had to fight to keep himself from hating these people for, once that hate took him by the throat, he knew that the killing would swiftly follow. It was in the very late afternoon of the second day that Hal Dozier came hurriedly to his shop, Hal Dozier with a drawn face of excitement.

"I got a surprise for you, Andy," he said. "Come along."

Andrew followed sluggishly to the door of the marshal's office. The marshal here bent to do something to his right spur

"Go on in, Andy. I'll follow right on as soon as I get this spur fixed."

Andy mechanically opened the office door and stood slouched against the wall. A full moment elapsed before he sensed another presence in the room and came suddenly erect, his nerves twitching. He turned, fighting himself to make the motion slow, and then he saw her. She was rising from her chair, big eyed, as if she doubted her reception, half smiling, as if she hoped for happiness. She was more flowerlike than ever, he thought, and her beauty struck him with a soul-stirring surprise, as something remembered, and yet with all the exquisite details forgotten. The difference between Anne Withero remembered and Anne Withero present was the difference between a dream and reality.

His eyes went down to the slender hand and the bending fingers that rested on the table. He found nothing to say, but he shut the door, always keeping his hungry eyes on her. And now Anne grew afraid, for she was looking at a new man, not the smooth-cheeked, careless, fire-eyed youth she remembered, but a man stamped with a starved look of suffering and dull, melancholy eyes.

At last she managed to say: "You wouldn't come to me,

The Return of Free Range Lanning

you know, and so I had to come to you, Andrew."

"Oh, Anne," he whispered, "are you real? Is it you?"

"Of course! But, Andy, you've been terribly sick."

"That's all past, and. . . ."

They seemed to fumble their way around the table, as if they were walking in sleep.

"You've kept one touch of belief in me, Anne?"

"Kept it? Ah, don't you see that I've never doubted you even?"

This much the marshal heard, for he had stayed guiltily near the door but, at this point, he was mastered by a decent respect for the rights of lovers and walked reluctantly away. It was still terribly hot, but the sheriff took off his hat to the full blaze of the slant sun and smiled, as if a cool breeze were playing on his face.

Dozier came back after what he thought was a painfully long time, and found them sitting close together, their dim, frightened eyes avoiding each other. The marshal was one of those lucky men who keep close to their youth, and his heart jumped at what he saw. He even understood when Andy Lanning rose and strode out of the room without a word to either of them.

The marshal closed the door after him and stood fanning himself with his hat and grinning shamelessly at Anne Withero. He liked her blush, and he liked her dignity, and he admired a poise that enabled her to smile back at him, as if she knew that he understood.

"If you knew," he said at last, "what it means to me. That kid has been a load that's nearly busted my back. And now it's settled."

"But it isn't, you know," said Anne Withero, growing anxious again.

"You mean to say that, after you've come, he doesn't know that he has to go straight?"

"You see," she explained, fully as worried as the marshal, but determined to make Andrew logical and plausible, "he feels that he hasn't gone through a sufficient test. There is a bit of wildness in him, you know, Mister Dozier."

"Not much more than there is in a hawk," said the marshal dryly. "But what mischief is he up to now?"

"I tried to make him feel that he has been tested sufficiently. I told him that I knew about his meeting with the terrible man who struck him, and what a glorious thing I thought it was that he had endured it, and he wouldn't agree. He says that he came within an inch of doing something terrible. And he wants a little time still, you see, to make these stupid people accept him. He says that if he could do something that would make half a dozen of these men about the village come to him and shake hands with him, then he'd feel that he had restored himself, and then he would be willing to go anywhere."

"Even East with you?" asked the marshal, still dryly. "And do you agree with this infernal nonsense?"

"I think Andrew knows best," said Anne gravely.

Chapter Eleven
A Coat in the Corner

The existence of Martindale was peaceful enough, but it contained citizens who habitually slept with only one eye closed. Some of these men were wakened in the middle of the night by a dull, muffled noise, as if a vast volume of tightly compressed air had suddenly expanded to its full limits. The sound was strange enough to bring them out of bed, and among them was Hal Dozier, buckling on his gun as he ran. Other figures scurried down the street, and presently an outcry guided him through the moonlight to the bank.

The door was open and a dozen people were gathered in the room around the wrecked safe. The empty steel drawers were scattered here and there. The marshal cast one glance at it.

"Neat work," he murmured. "If it weren't for facts, I'd say Allister had a hand there. What you found, boys?"

"This!" They threw a coat to him. "We found this in the corner."

The marshal looked it over carelessly, then stiffened. "This!" he exclaimed chokingly.

"That's Andy Lanning's coat," said Si Hulan importantly. "Murder will out, Hal. We've got your fine bird at last."

"Go look in his shack," said the marshal, sick at heart.

He could not understand it. More than once he had seen the impulse to break the law, dammed up in a man like water swelling in the banks of a stream, burst forth at the most unlooked for moment. But Andrew Lanning had nothing in common with the criminally inclined law-

221

breaker. All the man's impulses were for honesty, and the marshal knew that Anne Withero alone, in any case, should have been a sufficient motive to have held the boy to his self-imposed discipline of moral regeneration. He shook his head in sad perplexity.

Two or three in the crowd had run down the street toward the Lanning house. The marshal trotted across to his office, firing orders that sent the rest of the crowd in haste for saddles and horses. It was the newly installed telephone that brought the marshal to his office but, with his hand on the receiver, he was stopped by a shouting farther up the street. The outcries shot down on the far side of the town and then veered up the valley.

Hal Dozier ran to his door to be met there by half a dozen excited men.

"We found him sitting on his bunk, pretending he'd just heard the noise and was dressing to go out to see what was the matter. Cool, eh? Hulan shoved a gun under his nose, and he put up his hands and looked dazed. Good actor, he is. Then we told him what had happened, that we'd found his coat, and that we had him dead to rights. He looks over at a chair by the window, as if he'd just missed the coat that minute.

" 'That's what they've done to get even!' he says.

"We told him to lead up to the money first.

" 'All right,' he said. 'Right outside.'

"Looked as though he was going along easy and peaceable. Then, as he turned for the door, he made a flick of his hand and knocked the gun out of Hulan's hand and dived into the rest of us. He went through us like an eel through water. I got my hands on him, but he busted loose, strong as steel.

"He ran out, and we jumped our hosses and started after. Looked easy to run him down while he was on foot. But he let out a whistle, and that mare of his come tearing out of the shed and run alongside of him. Up he jumps on her back, as easy as you please, and away down the valley. Two or three of the boys headed after him."

The Return of Free Range Lanning

Dozier heard this with the pain slowly dying out of his face and a red rage coming in its place.

"Boys," he said at the conclusion of the tale, "this is the end of the great Andrew Lanning. He's taken the valley road with the fastest hoss that ever ran in the mountains, but they's one thing faster than hossflesh."

He tapped the shoulder of Si Hulan.

"Hulan, you've got sense. Use it now. Get onto that telephone and ring Long Bridge. Tell them what's happened. Tell them that I'm chasing Lanning with a half dozen men. I want Long Bridge to send me men if they please. Above all, I want good hosses, and I want them ready and waiting before the morning, on the other side of the hills. They'll have lots of time to get them together. I want hosses more'n I want men. You make sure you tell them that. I'm going to run Lanning down with relays.

"After we get the fresh hosses from Long Bridge, we'll send a man with the played-out hosses back to Long Bridge to wire on to Glenwood. He can tell them where the hunt is heading and where to meet us with a second relay. Sally is a great hoss, but she can't outlast three sets of hosses. We'll catch her this side of the Cumberlands. Now, the rest of you that want to follow, come along. We got to ride tonight as we never rode before, and the end of our trail is the end of Lanning."

The marshal had spoken the truth when he said that there was no horse in the mountains that could pace with Sally, and it was never shown so clearly as on this night. With her master riding bareback and without bridle, guided only by the touch of his hand on one side of her neck or the other, she went down the only easy way out of Martindale, the long, narrow gorge that shot north into the mountains. She flew along well within her strength, but it was a dizzy pace for the three stanch little cow ponies that followed, and they dropped rapidly to the rear. Lanning became a flickering shape in the moon haze ahead, and finally that shape went out.

After that they drew their horses back to a canter to wait for the main body of the pursuit to overtake them.

They were courageous men enough, but three to one were not sufficient odds when one man was Andrew Lanning.

The clatter of many hoofs down the ravine announced the coming of the marshal. The thick of the posse overtook the forerunners on a rise in the floor of the valley, and they told briefly of what they had seen and done.

The marshal cursed briefly and effectively. They should have pressed boldly on, for the respite they gave Lanning would enable him to pause at the first ranch house for a saddle and bridle and, worst of all, a rifle. When the first house loomed out of the night, Dozier urged his men on ahead and dropped back himself to exchange a word with the people of the house. He was well enough mounted to overtake the rest.

He had hardly tapped at the door without dismounting, when the rancher appeared, revolver in hand.

"And who now?" he asked furiously.

"Dozier," said the marshal. "Who's passed this way?"

"Lanning and four men ahead of him."

"Four men ahead of him! Who were they?"

"Don't know. They didn't stop, and they rode as if they was careless about what become of the hossflesh. But Lanning stopped long enough to grab my best saddle. Stuck me up with a gun and stood over me while I done the saddling for him, and then he got my rifle."

The marshal waited to hear no more but rode on with a groan. Mounted on Sally bareback, with a revolver strapped to his hip, Lanning was formidable enough but, with a rifle in addition and a comfortable saddle beneath him, the difficulties of the task were doubled and redoubled.

Who the four men might be he had no idea. It was not common for four men to be riding furiously through the night and the mountains, but he had no time to juggle ideas. Lanning rode ahead, and Lanning was his goal.

When he regained the posse, Lanning had still not been sighted. The mountains on either side of the ravine now dwindled away and grew small, and it was possible that

The Return of Free Range Lanning

Andrew might have turned aside at almost any place. But something told Dozier that the fugitive would hold on due north. That was the easiest way, and in that direction Sally's dazzling speed would most avail the rider. Accordingly, the marshal urged his men to the fullest speed of their horses.

One thing at least was in his favor if he had guessed the route of Lanning. The fugitive would hold Sally back for a long chase, not thinking that the marshal would run his horses out in the first twenty miles, but that was exactly what Dozier would do. At the end of the twenty miles the fresh mounts from Long Bridge would be waiting for his men.

The first light of dawn came when they labored over the crest of the range and, as they pitched down toward the plain below, he picked out his men with shrewd glances. No one had joined who was not sure of his endurance or of his ability with weapons, for men knew that the trail of Andrew Lanning would not be child's play, no matter what the odds. Dozier gauged them carefully and nodded his content.

A strange happiness rose in him. This was the continuation, after so long a gap, of the pursuit in which he had ridden Gray Peter to death in the chase of Sally and the outlaw. And this second time he could not fail. It was not man against man, or horse against horse, but the law against a criminal who must die.

If only he had been right in his guess as to Lanning's direction! When the dawn brightened, he saw, far away across the plain, a solitary dark spot. He fastened his glasses on the moving object and made sure; then he swept the lower slopes of the hills and found the huddling group of fresh horses which had been sent out from Long Bridge.

The marshal communicated his tidings to the men and, with a yell, they spurred on the last of the first relay.

Chapter Twelve
"The Last Lap"

They changed horses and saddles swiftly, eager to be off on the fresh run. The marshal sent back to Long Bridge a message to telephone ahead to Glenwood to send out a fresh relay that must wait anywhere under the foot of the Cumberlands. Then he spurred on after his men.

Freshly mounted, they were urging their horses on at a killing pace, and presently the small form of Lanning began to come back to them slowly and surely. Twenty weary miles were behind Sally, and she could not stand against this new challenge. Yet stand she did! A fabulous tale at which he had often laughed came back to the marshal's mind, a tale of some half-bred Arabian pony which had done a hundred miles through mountains between twilight and dawn. But the endurance of Sally seemed to make the tale possible.

By the time the day was bright and the light could be seen flashing on the silken flanks of Sally, they had drawn perilously close to her, but from that point on she began to increase her lead. Once or twice in the morning the marshal stopped his own mount for a breath and, when he trained his glasses on the great mare, he could see her running smoothly, evenly, with none of the roll and lurch in her stride that tells of the weary horse. And then he called to his men and urged them to save the strength of their mounts. The greatest speed over the greatest distance, between that point and the first hills of the Cumberlands, that was what was wanted. There the second relay, which would surely run Lanning into the ground, would be waiting. That was fifteen miles away, and the blue Cumberlands were rolling vast and beautiful into the middle of the sky.

Toward the end of the stretch they had to send their ponies on at a killing pace, for Sally was slowly and surely drawing away. A sturdy gray dropped with a broken heart before that run was over, and still Sally went on to a greater lead and disappeared into the first hills of the Cumberlands.

But five minutes later the posse, weary, drawn-faced, ferociously determined, was on the fresh horses from Glenwood. They scattered out in a long line and charged the hills where Lanning had disappeared. Presently someone on the far left caught sight and drew in the others with a yell. That was the beginning of the hottest part of the struggle.

Nearly forty miles of running lay behind her, but Sally drew now on some mysterious reserve of strength which only those who know the generous hearts of fine horses can vaguely understand. The hilly country, too, was in her favor, and she took short cuts as nimbly as a goat. In spite of that, they pressed closer and closer. Before the middle of the morning came the crisis. Hal Dozier came in distant range, halted his horse, pitched his rifle to his shoulder, and tried three shots.

They fell wide of the mark. After half an hour more of riding he called for a volley. It was given with a will. Dozier, watching through his glass like a general directing artillery fire, saw the hat jump and fall lopsided on the head of Lanning, and yet he did not fall, but turned in his saddle. Three times his rifle spoke in quick succession, and three little puffs of rock dust jumped before three of the men of the posse. Dozier cursed in admiration.

"It's his way of telling us that he could have potted the three of you if he had wanted," he said. "Now spread out and ride like the wind."

They spread out and spurred obediently, fighting their horses up the slopes, which increased in difficulty, for they were nearing the heart of the Cumberlands. Sally still drifted just outside of close rifle fire. And eventually, about noon, she began to gain again. Hal Dozier shook his head in despair. Plainly the gallant mare must be traveling on her nerve strength alone, but how long it would last no one could tell.

He called his men back to a steady pace. They could only hope to get at Lanning now by wearing him down and reaching him by night. Certainly Sally would not last so long as that.

The afternoon came unendurably hot, with the men drooping and drowsy in their saddles from the long ride. It was at this time that they were jerked erect by the clang of three rapid shots, echoing a little distance ahead of them. They rounded the shoulder of the next hill hastily and saw the glistening form of Sally disappearing over a crest beyond, but in the hollow beneath them stood a horse with empty saddle, and the rider was lying prone beside it, his face exposed to the burning of the sun. Hal Dozier headed the rush into the hollow and dismounted.

It was Scottie who lay there, and Scottie had ridden his last ride. He begged for water feebly, but after it was given to him he spoke more clearly, and they made a futile pretext of binding his wounds. One bullet had smashed his right shoulder. The other had pierced his body below the lungs, and he was in agony from it, but he made no complaint. Death was coming quickly on him. Hal Dozier hurried the posse on and remained holding the head of the dying man.

"It was Lanning," murmured Scottie. "We blew the safe, Hal, and we planted Lanning's coat there to fix the blame on him. Then we started out."

"You were the four men on horses," said the marshal. "But how did you keep ahead of Sally? And why did Lanning take after you?"

"We used Allister's old gag," said Scottie. "We planted relays before we turned the trick. Then we lit out in a semicircle. But Lanning, he must have known that we turned that trick and threw the blame on him, remembered that we had an old meeting place up yonder in the

Cumberlands. And while we rode in an arc, he cut across in a straight line from Martindale, and Sally brought him up to us.

"We saw him following. We could see you following Andy. A game of tag, eh? The devil played against us, however. I cursed Sally till my throat was dry. There's no wear-out to that mare! She kept coming on at us. Finally we drew up and gave our nags a breath and drew straws to see who should go back and try to pot Lanning. I got the short straw, and I went back. Well, it was a game of tag, and I'm it."

He added after a moment: "But while it lasted . . . a great game. S'long, Hal."

He died without a murmur of pain, without a convulsion of face or body and, to the very end, he kept an iron grip on himself.

Hal Dozier rode like mad to the posse and communicated his tidings. The real criminals rode far beyond. The man they chased was acting the part of a skirmisher. They must ride now, not to kill Lanning, but to keep him from being overpowered by the numbers.

It was a singular goal for that posse, but they were sharpened by the phrase: "The last of old Allister's gang."

They rode hard, using the last strength of their horses. Two hours wore on, but there was no sight of Sally again. It was a strange predicament. The more they pressed on Lanning, the more he would struggle to escape and close on the real criminals. And yet they could not desist and leave odds of three to one against him, and such odds!

At last they were riding over gravel and hard rock that gave no trail to follow. Suddenly a second fusillade made them spur their horses on. The crackling of guns had been far away, only a gust of wind had blown the sound to them, showing how hopelessly they had been distanced. They urged their sweating horses on in the ominous silence that followed the firing. Then the neighing of a horse guided them.

They climbed to a ridge and, on the shoulder below them, in a natural theater rimmed by great rocks, they saw the picture. The gaunt, horrible body of Larry la Roche lay propped against the rocks, his long arms spread out beside him. Clune was curled up on his side nearby, with the gravel scuffed away where he had struggled in the death agony. In the center of the terrible little stage lay no less a person than Lefty Gruger, gaping at the sky, and across him lay the body of him who had worked all this death, Andrew Lanning. Above him, trembling with weariness, stood beautiful Sally, neighing for help till the mountainside reechoed.

Not a man spoke as they went down the slope.

The whole thing was perfectly clear. The gang, hard pressed by their terrible antagonist, had turned back and waylaid him, taking ambush behind these rocks. When he came down, they had shot him from his horse. It was while he was falling, perhaps, and while he lay on the ground that they had rushed him, but the revolver of Lanning had come out, and this was its work. The first bullet had slain the grim La Roche, and the second had curled up Clune. The head of Lefty Gruger had been smashed with a stroke of the butt as he came running to close quarters.

They lifted the form of the conqueror from the body of Lefty Gruger, and the marshal, with his face pressed to the breast of Andy, caught the faint flutter of the heart.

Only then they set about the work of first aid, and they started with a sort of fierce determination, hard eyed and drawnlipped. The marshal cursed them as they worked, telling them briefly the true story of Andrew Lanning, which they would never believe before. And now, it seemed, he had given his life for them.

It was a dubious matter indeed. The bullet that had knocked him from his horse had whipped through his thigh. Another had broken his left arm, and a third—and this was the dangerous one—had plowed straight through his body. When his breathing became perceptible, a red bubble rose to his lips. Somewhere that bullet had touched the lungs, and now the matter of life or death was as uncertain as the flip of a coin.

The Return of Free Range Lanning

They could not dream of removing him. He must be brought back to life, or die on the spot, and they worked like madmen, throwing a shelter against sun and wind above him, bedding him soft in saddle blankets and fir boughs, washing the wounds and bandaging them.

"Get the doctor from Glenwood," said Hal Dozier to his messengers, "and get Anne Withero . . . she's in Martindale. Let the doc come as fast as he can, but make Anne Withero come like the wind!"

The doctor was there before dark, and he shook his head.

Anne Withero was there before midnight, and she set her teeth.

At dawn the doctor admitted there was a ghost of a hope. At noon he declared for a fighting chance. In the twilight Andy Lanning parted his stained lips and whispered into the ear of Anne Withero: "The bad strain, dear . . . I think they've let it out."

Max Brand is the best-known pen name of Frederick Faust, creator of Dr. Kildare, Destry, and many other fictional characters popular with readers and viewers worldwide. Faust wrote for a variety of audiences in many genres. His enormous output, totaling approximately thirty million words or the equivalent of 530 ordinary books, covered nearly every field: crime, fantasy, historical romance, espionage, Westerns, science fiction, adventure, animal stories, love, war, and fashionable society, big business and big medicine. Eighty motion pictures have been based on his work along with many radio and television programs. For good measure he also published four volumes of poetry. Perhaps no other author has reached more people in more different ways.

Born in Seattle in 1892, orphaned early, Faust grew up in the rural San Joaquin Valley of California. At Berkeley he became a student rebel and one-man literary movement, contributing prodigiously to all campus publications. Denied a degree because of unconventional conduct, he embarked on a series of adventures culminating in New York City where, after a period of near starvation, he received simultaneous recognition as a serious poet and successful popular-prose writer. Later, he traveled widely, making his home in New York, then in Florence, and finally in Los Angeles.

Once the United States entered the Second World War, Faust abandoned his lucrative writing career and his work as a screenwriter to serve as a war correspondent with the infantry in Italy, despite his fifty-one years and a bad heart. He was killed during a night attack on a hilltop village held by the German army. New books based on magazine serials or unpublished manuscripts or restored versions continue to appear so that, alive or dead, he has averaged a new book every four months for seventy-five years. In the United States alone nine publishers now issue his work. Beyond this, some work by him is newly reprinted every week of every year in one or another format somewhere in the world. Yet, only recently have the full dimensions of this extraordinarily

The Return of Free Range Lanning

versatile and prolific writer come to be recognized and his stature as a protean literary figure in the twentieth century acknowledged. His popularity continues to grow throughout the world.

MAX BRAND

"Brand practices his art to something like perfection!"
—The New York Times

Red Devil of the Range. Only two things in this world are worth a damn to young Ever Winton—his Uncle Clay and the mighty Red Pacer, the wildest, most untamable piece of horseflesh in the West. Then in one black hour they are both gone—the notorious hardcase Timberline buys Red Pacer and the sheriff takes Uncle Clay away at gunpoint. Ever knows he has to get them both back, although that means selling his soul and riding with Timberline outside the law. He'll do whatever it takes, even if it costs his life—or somebody else's.

__4122-7 $4.50 US/$5.50 CAN

Pride of Tyson. The untamed frontier is a graveyard for cowardly greenhorns who can't outshoot, outwit, or outlast the human vultures who feed off their fear. But Henry Tyson has bitten off and spit out the silver spoon that is his birthright, and has been fighting ever since. Fleeing the life of a New York swell, he blazes a trail to the lawless land of renegades and rustlers, double-dealing gamblers and backshooting gringos. And he'll be damned if some gutless gunman is going to fill his belly with lead and leave his rotting corpse for a buzzard's banquet.

__4113-8 $4.50 US/$5.50 CAN

Dorchester Publishing Co., Inc.
65 Commerce Road
Stamford, CT 06902

Please add $1.75 for shipping and handling for the first book and $.50 for each book thereafter. NY, NYC, PA and CT residents, please add appropriate sales tax. No cash, stamps, or C.O.D.s. All orders shipped within 6 weeks via postal service book rate. Canadian orders require $2.00 extra postage and must be paid in U.S. dollars through a U.S. banking facility.

Name_____

Address_____

City _____ State_____Zip_____

I have enclosed $_____in payment for the checked book(s).
Payment <u>must</u> accompany all orders.□ Please send a free catalog.

THE TRAP AT COMANCHE BEND

FIRST TIME IN PAPERBACK!

"Brand is a topnotcher!"
—*New York Times*

Like a vulture descending on a rotting-corpse, Jerry Aiken can smell gold nuggets from a mile away, and he'll do anything to keep his pockets full. A cardsharp, a cattleman, a hired gun—he's tried every legal means in the West to strike the mother lode. It isn't until a wealthy Eastern dude offers him some easy money that Aiken strays outside the law.

All Jerry has to do is kidnap the rich man's daughter and scare some sense into her. But all hell breaks loose when the hellion heiress escapes. If Aiken can't get her back, the only reward he'll get will be a long stretch in the territorial hoosegow.

_3622-3 $3.99 US/$4.99 CAN